TALES FROM THE BLUE ROOM

TALES FROM THE BLUE ROOM
An Anthology of New Short Fiction

Peter Bunzl

Annette Caseley

Donald Clark

Ruth Cohen

Colin Harlow

Fleur Jeremiah

Edd Phillips

Paul Yates

First printed in 2014

Reprinted in 2014

ISBN-13: 978 0 9574919 1 5

Published by: Drew London LTD

Design and typesetting by: Drew London LTD

blueroomwriters@gmail.com

blueroomwriters.wordpress.com

The Little Bother Copyright © 2014 Peter Bunzl

Sarkovski's Tower Copyright © 2014 Donald Clark

Cosmo and Damian's Christmas Outing Copyright © 2014 Paul Yates

Time to be a Man Copyright © 2014 Edd Phillips

Vanamo Copyright © 2014 Fleur Jeremiah

The Shadow Copyright © 2014 Ruth Cohen

Flirting with Danger Copyright © 2014 Annette Caseley

Big Love Copyright © 2014 Colin Harlow

Whisky Chasers Copyright © 2014 Peter Bunzl

The Unicorn Copyright © 2014 Paul Yates

A Tidy Garden Copyright © 2014 Annette Caseley

The Way to a Man's Heart Copyright © 2014 Ruth Cohen

A Light Finger Buffet Copyright © 2014 Colin Harlow

The Committee Copyright © 2014 Fleur Jeremiah

I Never Thought That Could Happen Here Copyright © 2014 Donald Clark

This book or any portion thereof may not be reproduced or used in any manner whatsoever without the express written permission of the publisher except for the use of brief quotations in a book review. This is a work of fiction. Names, characters, businesses, places, events and incidents are either the products of the author's imagination or used in a fictitious manner. Any resemblance to actual persons, living or dead, or actual events is purely coincidental.

All rights reserved.

CONTENTS

The Little Bother *Peter Bunzl*	11	Whisky Chasers *Peter Bunzl*	107
Sarkovski's Tower *Donald Clark*	33	The Unicorn *Paul Yates*	125
Cosmo and Damian's Christmas Outing *Paul Yates*	47	A Tidy Garden *Annette Caseley*	149
Time to Be a Man *Edd Phillips*	63	The Way to a Man's Heart *Ruth Cohen*	161
Vanamo *Fleur Jeremiah*	73	A Light Finger Buffet *Colin Harlow*	169
The Shadow *Ruth Cohen*	83	The Committee *Fleur Jeremiah*	185
Flirting with Danger *Annette Caseley*	91	I Never Thought That Could Happen Here *Donald Clark*	201
Big Love *Colin Harlow*	99	Biographies	217

THE LITTLE BOTHER
Peter Bunzl

Ryan had read half his book, listened to all his music, eaten two packets of biscuits and an apple, played seventy-two games of *Donkey Kong*, completing all the levels, and counted every Italian sports car they'd passed in the last hundred miles. Twenty four hours of groggy sticky travel, twenty-four hours stuck in this overheated tin can on wheels, and he finally knew what it was like to be utterly and unendingly bored. He propped an elbow on the car window frame and stuck his arm out of the opening. Combing his hand through the slipstream, he let the cool air tickle his fingers as he watched the countryside stream past.

He was thinking about the many ways he could make the Little Bother's life a misery. The plethora of pain experiments he could conduct. Tortures. Two-handed Chinese burns. Forcing fingernails, or real nails, into flabby flesh. Perhaps pushing the Little Bother's fat thumbs back to the knuckles and twisting them to see what happened. Or punching his bothersome face with a fist. And after that, the aftermath – the little wails and tear-stained blubs. The bubbles of spit on the blood-soaked teeth. Soon as they stopped, soon as the Growns had their backs turned, he knew he'd do it. Do it just to see the look of surprise on the Little Bother's face.

'Not long now,' Mum told them. 'I think I've found where we are.'

Dad tapped the steering wheel. 'That's what you said when we turned off the motorway. We're not lost again, are we?' His rough bearded face, framed in the side mirror, had taken on a look of resigned frustration. Under the shadowy brim of his sunhat his gaze flicked between Mum and the road.

Mum pretended not to hear him and instead went back to studying the map. With one finger she traced the spaghetti tangle of Italian back roads, searching the folds for a recognizable landmark.

The Little Bother picked at a scab on his knee and looked up from the comic he was reading. 'You know when you jump on a girder,' he said to no one in particular, 'and there's another girder on the other end that goes flying?'

'You mean like in Mario, or something?' Ryan asked, not bothering to look round.

The Little Bother swung his sandalled feet back and forth, kicking his heels against the car seat as he considered this. 'I'm not talking about Super Mary-o-land, stupid. I'm talking about Superman.'

'It's *Super Mario Land*,' Ryan told the Little Bother. 'And, no, I don't know. I don't know what the fuck you're talking about.'

'Language!' Mum gave him a dose of the evil eye in the rear view mirror. 'Both of you, I want no more of your bickering today, OK?'

THE LITTLE BOTHER

Ryan nodded but when she was no longer watching he reached out and punched the Little Bother in the arm.

The Little Bother made a face like a sad cherub and rubbed his shoulder. 'You do know about the girders,' he whispered. 'You know because I told you.' And with that he slumped sideways, letting his head fall against the window.

Behind his halo of blond curls a column of poplars marched towards a tumble-down village; rows of leafy vines lolloped along the verge of the road; a dusty road sign whizzed past.

'This is it!' Mum said suddenly. 'This is our turning!'

Dad stamped on the brakes and yanked the wheel, shifting them on to a narrow gravel track.

'How about a little warning next time?'

'I can only tell you what's on the map.'

Mum gripped her door frame while the car bucked down a steep slope and into the bowl of the valley.

As they turned a corner and came out from behind a line of trees, Ryan caught a glimpse of the tiled roof of their new home nestled deep in the hillside and peeping out from behind a weeping willow.

'Here we are.' Dad tapped the brakes and brought the car coasting to a stop. Ryan and the Little Bother leaned forward and stared out of the insect encrusted windscreen.

A few feet in front of the car the track petered out and an earth path took over. Crossing a brown field littered with rocks and thistles, it headed towards a squat farmhouse whose rough stone walls stood shadowed against the early evening sky.

'Is that it?' Ryan asked.

Mum undid her seat belt. 'That's it, sweetheart.'

'It comes with twenty acres,' Dad said as he switched off the engine. 'We can grow our own vegetables.'

'Looks like a dump.'

'It's the simple life, that's all.' Mum folded the map and placed it on the dashboard then brushed the travel creases from her dress.

The Little Bother yawned and rubbed his eyes. 'So we're not going any further?'

'No, we're not going any further. The road ends here.' Dad pressed the button to release the central locking. He got out of the car and took his jacket from where it hung over his headrest. 'Well, come on then,' he said. 'Look lively!'

The four of them walked along the path spread out in a loose row. As they approached the house the building seemed to turn away from them, revealing a side wall that was covered in Virginia creeper. There was no gate. Instead the fence ended in a tangle of wires, its posts fallen like drunks into the brambles at the base of a line of olive trees.

They crossed a yard of broken farm implements and took a set of shallow steps up to a rotten porch. Here they found a collection of horseshoes nailed around the front door and, hanging on a hook, a piece of curved metal that was longer than Ryan's arm and filled with rusty teeth.

The Little Bother put out a finger and touched it. 'This is Ironman's mouth,' he told them. 'And this is his toe.'

He kicked over a dead plant in a pot. It bounced down the steps and rolled across the yard.

'That's nice, dear,' Mum said, 'but don't touch.'

'There's lots to see,' Dad said, and they stood and waited while he searched through a big ring of keys, trying each until he found the one that unlocked the front door.

The hall smelt musty and damp – the smell of a place where the windows haven't been opened for years. Unloved and unlived in. They climbed the stairs to the first-floor landing. There was no rail, just a frayed rope, and the thick whitewashed walls were bumpy and cold to the touch. Another door: Dad fumbled with its lock and then they stepped into the farmhouse proper and surveyed the scene.

Their furniture was stacked under a patched tarpaulin at the centre of a large gloomy room. Ryan could make out the lumpy shapes of three beds, a row of chairs and their old kitchen table, a corner of which stuck out from underneath the tarp. A thick layer of dust covered the rest of the space and it looked as if someone had gone at the walls with a jack hammer. Deep channels chased along the expanse of pockmarked plaster, across exposed stonework, and up to the large wooden beams that held up the pitched roof.

'You sold our house in London for this?' Ryan asked.

'Of course,' Mum said. 'We discussed it, remember? It's our dream home.' Her smile was unconvincing.

Dad tried the light switch, but it didn't work. 'Doesn't seem like they've put the electric wiring in yet,' he said.

'Probably been too busy with the septic tank.'

'What's a septic tank?' the Little Bother asked.

'It's the place where all your shit goes,' Ryan said.

Mum ran a hand through her ragged hair. 'Didn't I tell you before to mind your language in front of him?'

Ryan ignored her. He stepped over to the door and drew a smiley in the dust on its back panel with one finger, then wiped it away. When he examined his palm it was covered in a tidemark of filth. 'Where's this dust come from anyhow?' he asked.

'From sanding the roof beams,' Dad said. He was inspecting one of the larger holes in the wall.

Mum watched him for a moment, then sighed and gave a slow despairing shake of her head. 'It's gone everywhere. I thought you told the builders to clear up before we arrived?'

Dad shrugged. 'I don't think they understood my Italian. Never mind. We'll soon have it shipshape. There's a bucket and some cloths in the car. The boys'll help me get them in, won't you, boys?'

He tried to put a hand on Mum's arm, but she brushed it away. Stepping over to the shutters, she pulled them open and stared out of the grimy window at the fading light.

'Oh, love,' she said. 'What have we done?'

Somewhere across the valley a dog began to bark.

Ryan and the Little Bother waited in the field, among the rocks and thistles, while Dad opened the boot of the car and searched through the luggage for the bucket of cleaning stuff. Above him a flight of swallows circled in the red sky; from time to time one would dive from the group and disappear behind the line of olive trees.

'Self-sufficiency, you see?' Dad said as he pulled out various bags and boxes. 'It's a skill. A skill most people today don't have, but you'll learn it. We all will.'

The Little Bother nodded. A mangy looking cat stalked past them and Ryan watched as it lay down beside the tangle of wire and fence posts and proceeded to lick its balls.

After a minute the Little Bother poked at Ryan's arm. 'You didn't answer my question from earlier,' he said.

'What question?' Ryan asked.

'The one where you're running and you take off and fly in the air and do a double somersault and land on your feet.'

'That's not the same question,' Ryan said.

'This is a new one now,' said the Little Bother. 'Have you ever done it?'

'Why do you care so much what I've done?'

'It's important.'

Ryan shook his head. 'No one has, except maybe one of those Olympic gymnasts.'

The Little Bother gave a knowing smile, stuck a fat finger in his nose and wiggled it about. 'Superman has. And so have I.'

'You have not,' Ryan told him. He scratched the pit of his chest with a hand. His shirt, damp with the sweat of the day, had started to feel cold against his skin.

'I have,' the Little Bother said again.

'Yeah, right. When?'

'All the time. You've just never seen me do it because it's when you're not looking.' The Little Bother widened his stupid blue eyes to show he was telling the truth. It was a trick Ryan had taught him and he was definitely getting better at it, but that wouldn't save him when the time came for revenge.

'Here they are! I've found them.' Dad pulled the bucket of cloths and a camping lamp out from the back of the car. 'Thank God for that! I thought for a moment we'd left them behind.'

The light had nearly gone as they walked back to the house and all about the field frogs croaked to each other in the expanding darkness. Dad carried two large suitcases, one under each arm. Ryan clasped a third smaller one, along with the hissing gas lamp, which he held out in front of his face to illuminate the path. It glowed with a warm pulsing yellow light that made odd shadows jump between the broken farm implements of the yard.

The Little Bother carried the bucket, swinging it back and forth ferociously. 'It's too dark,' he whispered as they entered the house and climbed the stairs.

'Don't worry,' Dad said. 'We'll soon have the electrics working.'

'Soon as hell freezes over,' Ryan muttered.

Mum was still standing where they'd left her, staring out of the open window, her hand hovered in the air, a half-smoked cigarette clasped between her fingers.

Dad put down the bags. 'I didn't know you were smoking again.'

'Can you blame me under the circumstances?' She crushed the butt on the sill and threw it out into the darkness. 'Right then,' she said, gathering up all her efficiency. 'Let's get started.'

They took the tarpaulin off the furniture and found it was caked in dust too. So they turned over the mattresses on the beds and wiped the chairs and the table down with a cloth, which immediately turned the same grey colour as everything else.

'I suppose we'd should clean the floor,' Mum said wearily. 'We don't want it getting over everything in the suitcases.' She sat down on the edge of a bed. 'Do you think it's too much to hope that they've turned the water on?'

Dad took his jacket off and placed it over the back of a chair. 'I'll go and find out, shall I?'

'Yes, perhaps you might?' Mum's voice was beginning to crack with the effort of being civil.

'Come on then, boys.'

Dad ushered Ryan and the Little Bother back into the corridor and then through another room that was filled with unidentifiable Italian furniture, all brown and heavy with a patina of mildew. They stepped through an archway curtained with plastic beads and found themselves in a narrow galley kitchen, where a cooker and a blue gas cylinder stood beside a single cupboard. Dad took the bucket from the Little Bother and put it in a large stone sink.

'Can I have some light over here please?' he asked, and Ryan held the lamp over the sink while he turned on the tap.

They waited but nothing came. Thirty seconds passed, and then finally an eruption of clanking emerged from the walls, shot along the pipes and burst from the mouths of the taps in a loud groan. A thin stream of water spurted into the base of the bucket, filling it slowly in squirts and dribbles.

'It sounds like the house is taking a piss,' Ryan said.

'You mean a leak?' The Little Bother scratched the tip of his ear and glanced over at a stack of bricks in the corner. 'Do you think you could karate chop one of those in half?' he asked Ryan.

'What are you on about now?' Ryan said.

'When you use your hand to hit through a brick. Have you ever done that?'

'No, but I suppose you have?'

'Loads of times.'

Ryan sighed. 'How did I guess,' he said. His arm was starting to ache with the effort of holding up the lamp. 'And why are you asking me all these dumb questions?'

'It's a superhero test. I made it up. You know when you stand on the roof of a house and put your arms out to fly –'

'Do you know what?' Ryan interrupted. 'I think you might be retarded.'

'I'm what?' asked the Little Bother.

'Retarded. You know, when your brain doesn't work and –'

'Dad, what's retarded?'

'Did you call him retarded?' Dad asked.

'No.'

'Don't use words like that.'

'I won't if you get him to shut up,' Ryan said. 'He's been going on about all this for hours.'

Dad turned toward the Little Bother, the shadows lifting from his face in the glare of the lamp. 'Why don't you leave Ryan alone for a bit now, OK, little man?'

'OK.'

'And, both of you, try not to upset your mother this evening.'

'Why?' the Little Bother asked.

'Just because,' Dad said.

'Because Dad's done that already,' Ryan said.

'That's enough now.'

When the bucket was finally full Dad looked under the sink and found an old bottle of washing up liquid. He squirted the dregs of it into the water and then threw in the cloths.

***

Back in the main room Mum took charge and they each chose a different corner and began to clean. The floorboards were caked in a thick layer of polish that held on to the dust and they ended up going over them multiple times, soon Ryan's arm ached and his bare knuckles had turned red from all the effort of cleaning.

'Do you think superheroes can live in Italy?' the Little Bother asked.

Mum looked up from ringing out her cloth in the bucket. 'I don't see why not,' she said.

'It's just I've never heard of an Italian superhero before.'

'Neither have I, but maybe if you were Italian you would have.'

'Like what?' the Little Bother asked.

She thought for a moment. 'I don't know, maybe Spaghetti-Man.'

'What's his special power?'

'Tangling people up in spaghetti.'

The Little Bother laughed. 'I like that,' he said.

'Hey! That could be you,' Ryan said. 'You could be Spaghetti-Man. Or Mr Meatball. Or just the Little Bother.' The Little Bother froze when he heard that one. 'That's it!' Ryan said. 'That's your superhero name – the Little Bother, because you go round pestering people till they can't take it and then they die because their mind's melted away from all the crud you talk.'

'Shut up. That's not who I am,' the Little Bother said. 'I'm the Big Bother. I'm the Big Bother because I stop as much crime as all the superheroes put together. And everyone says: "Look out! Here comes the Big Bother!"'

'You're the Big Bother because you're so annoying,' Ryan said.

'For God's sake!' Dad shouted. 'Be quiet, both of you. I've just about had enough of your bickering.'

The Little Bother threw down his cloth. 'I don't want to do this any more,' he complained. 'It's dark and my hand's gone wrinkly.'

'Mine too,' Ryan said.

'All right,' Dad said. 'I'll tell you what. Why don't we call it a night? We can take the car and get some dinner.'

Mum stood and threw her cloth into the bucket. 'I think,' she said, 'that that would be a very good idea.'

They drove to the nearest town and walked around for a bit, looking at the grey stone buildings and the closed shutters of the shops. The Little Bother had cheered up remarkably and was now playing an improvised game of hopscotch on the old paving stones and singing a song about frogs.

Finally they found somewhere that was still open: a little takeaway pizza place under the arched entrance of the old wall. There they brought four squares of pizza with ham, mushrooms and mozzarella, and the man behind the counter laid each slice on a piece of greaseproof paper for them. Then they sat in companionable silence on the high stools in the window and ate the warm tomatoey bread, hand to mouth, in big greedy bites, while in the background tinny Italian pop music played on the radio; and the fridge hummed; and the neon lights buzzed off the white-tiled walls.

When they got back Mum found some sheets shoved in her suitcase and since it was too late now to move the beds to the other rooms they made them up where they were. Afterwards they lined up in the kitchen and brushed their teeth at the sink, before they all trooped back to their beds and Dad turned off the gas lamp.

Even with the shutters and the windows open the room was warm and it took Ryan a long while to get to sleep. He lay listening to the sounds of the night – the Little Bother's occasional murmur beside him, the light whistle of Mum's breath, Dad's snoring – and, beyond that, the silence. A silence as pitch black as the countryside. A silence that smothered all thoughts of the world and the city and the friends he'd left behind.

* * *

The next morning Ryan woke to find the sun and the Little Bother both trying to tickle his feet. When he finally got up there were all sorts of chores that needed doing, and it was nearly midday before he finished helping the Growns with cleaning and moving the furniture. After that he and the Little Bother were finally allowed out to explore the grounds with Mum's proviso that they kept an eye on each other, or rather, that he, Ryan, kept an eye on the Little Bother.

Starting in the yard, they walked slowly in an anticlockwise direction, picking their way around the house.

Low crumbling outbuildings clung like limpets to the external walls of the farm and Ryan opened each of their doors in turn so they could peer in at the earthen floors and cobwebbed walls.

They found derelict pigsties filled with broken water troughs and cellars of rusty discarded tools. Barns and basements and moss-cracked brick rooms, musty with the smell of straw dust and animal shit.

'Look at all this junk,' Ryan said. 'Who knows what it's for?'

'Farming,' the Little Bother said.

'They don't know the first thing about farming. They won't last five minutes here. By this time next week we'll be back in England.'

The Little Bother bit his lip and looked at Ryan as if he'd committed sacrilege. 'We're staying. Mum says so. Besides, I like it.'

'You would,' Ryan said.

On the far side of the house, still in shadow, something had left the entrails of a small dead animal – probably a lizard – in little gobbets around the yard. The ants were already all over them, streaming back and forth in long black lines.

The Little Bother crouched down and picked up a stick; with the thin end he poked at an ant carrying a fatty globule. 'Do you think they eat those bits?' he asked.

'I don't know and I don't care,' Ryan said. 'Why don't you leave them alone?' He caught the Little Bother by the arm and yanked him up, pulling him towards a vaulted cellar.

When he opened the door to push the Little Bother inside there was a snake spread across the floor. A long green scaly squiggle, framed in the square of light. It lifted its head and hissed at him, staring him down with black beady eyes. Ryan was so shocked he let go of the Little Bother and let out a strangled cry; and the Little Bother laughed as the creature darted off through a crack in the wall.

'You were scared,' he told Ryan.

And Ryan looked into his fat face and saw that this information had power, so he punched the Little Bother in the arm.

'No, I wasn't,' he said. 'You were.'

They walked on downhill and came across an old brick water tank, set into the hillside, and as they approached it the insects sat chattering round the edges scattered away into the long grass.

The tank was filled by a trickle of water from a rusty metal pipe sticking out of a rock and emptied by a grooved parapet at the other end, where the overflow cascaded into a brick channel that ran along the edge of the field. The front wall of the tank was encased with a thick green crust of algae that became a slimy porridge of weed when it reached the water's surface. Ryan dipped a hand in the tank and swirled the weed, spiralling it around. He raked out a handful and threw it on to the ground and it dried quickly in the sun, hardening into snotty green lumps.

'You know it'll take years for them to fix this place up,' Ryan told the Little Bother. 'Remember how long it took them to fix up our old house? And they started that before you were even born.'

'So?' The Little Bother rubbed his arm where Ryan had hit him.

Somewhere across the valley a tractor started up, its engine echoing around the hillside in a mechanical drone.

'So nothing. I'm just telling you the truth, that's all. You'll probably be dead before they finish here.'

'Don't say things like that.'

'It's true.' Ryan wiggled his fingers in the water. Beneath their pink tips black tadpoles swam to and fro. 'You'll probably be working on this farm for the rest of your days. And even then it won't be finished.'

'Dad says it'll be done next year.'

Ryan gave a short sarcastic laugh. 'It won't be. Especially with you around causing bother.'

'You'll be here too.'

'I'm out of here as soon as possible,' Ryan said. 'Soon as I'm sixteen, I'm gone.'

The Little Bother wiped a hand across his face. 'You are not,' he said. 'And why do you always say I cause bother? It's not nice.'

'You're the most bothersome person I know.' Ryan grabbed a fistful of the snot-weed and rubbed it on the Little Bother's head.

'Oww! Don't do that. It hurts.'

The Little Bother pulled another clump of weed from the pond and threw it at Ryan. It hit him square across the chest and he retaliated by grabbing the Little Bother's arm and rubbing more weed in his face.

'Retard!' the Little Bother shouted, and he pushed Ryan away and ran off crying.

'You're the retard!' Ryan shouted after him. 'Where are you going, retard?'

He wandered through the hanging fronds of the weeping willow, batting them apart so that they closed curtain-like behind him, but he could not find the Little Bother.

* * *

That evening a thunderstorm broke across the valley. Dark clouds crowded the sky and forked tongues of lightning licked across the tips of the far hills. Ryan washed his hair in the kitchen sink by sticking his head under the taps and holding it there. Out of the corner of his eye he could see a cracked brown stain around the plughole that looked suspiciously like the outline of a dead spider.

At dinner he watched the Little Bother sucking up pasta. The white worms wiggling as they disappeared into his mouth, tomato sauce flicking around his lips. The Little Bother had a Superman comic open beside his plate and as he read he picked pieces of the dried snot-weed from his hair with his free hand and smeared them across the underside of the table.

'We saw a snake today,' the Little Bother said, when he'd finally finished eating. 'A big green one.'

'Oh, I forgot to tell you about those.' Dad topped up the wine in his chipped glass. 'When the house was derelict it must have moved in. Probably thought it had found a new home!'

Ryan pushed his chair back from the table, rocking it up on its back legs. 'The house is still derelict,' he muttered under his breath.

'Are the snakes here dangerous?' the Little Bother asked.

Mum wiped her plate with a hunk of bread and popped it in her mouth. 'Not the green ones,' she said. 'They're just grass snakes.'

'But watch out for the black ones,' Dad added. 'They're deadly vipers.' He held his index fingers up to his mouth like fangs and hissed at the Little Bother.

The Little Bother gave a wild cackle. 'Will they come in the house?'

'Not now they know we're here,' Dad said. 'Snakes keep to the long grass, away from people, and they're easily startled, so remember to make lots of noise when you walk. But I don't need to tell you that, right? Right?'

He leaned round the table and grabbed the Little Bother, tickling him under his armpits until he wriggled with glee.

'Seriously, though, both of you,' Mum said, 'if you see one you're not to go near it and if you get bitten come and tell us straight away.'

'Because we'll turn into Snakemen?' the Little Bother asked.

Mum laughed. 'No, because we'll have to go to the hospital for serum.'

Dad was still holding on to the Little Bother, hugging him. 'Anyway,' he said, 'they're probably more scared of you than you are of them.'

'He was the scaredest,' said the Little Bother. 'A big scardey cat.'

'No I wasn't.'

Dad put out his free hand to ruffle Ryan's hair. 'Don't be scared, son,' he said. 'Just be careful.'

'I'm not,' Ryan told him. 'I will be.'

'Do you want to be part of my gang?' the Little Bother asked him the next day.

'Not really,' Ryan said.

He was sat on a high stone wall that encompassed an old orchard of apple trees. Their hard little buds had turned verdant green after the storm. This orchard was as far from the house as Ryan could get, but even so the Little Bother had found him. He stood there with his arms folded over his blue T-shirt, waiting for an answer. In the frame of Ryan's sunglasses his face looked almost pink.

'What does being in this gang involve?' Ryan asked finally.

'Fighting crime and stuff, like Superman,' the Little Bother said, as if it was the most obvious thing in the world.

'Here?' Ryan tipped back his cap and looked around.

'Yes. This could be our secret hideout.'

'How so?'

'Because no one knows about it,' the Little Bother said, 'so we could go out at night and fight criminals.'

Somewhere in the trees a hoopoe was calling. Across the valley another answered it. Ryan scratched his leg. A rash of red mosquito bites had started to bloom around his ankle.

'Where are you going to find crime in the middle of the countryside?' he asked.

The Little Bother clasped his hands behind him, pushing them up and away like he was doing a gym stretch. 'There are villains everywhere,' he said. 'Don't you know that?'

'You read too many comics,' Ryan said. 'Besides you can't fight criminals, you've got no powers.'

By his leg a lizard stuck its head from a crack and scooted across the stones, before disappearing over the parapet.

'I can too fight,' the Little Bother said.

'Really? Prove it.'

'I have to be ready.'

'Yeah? Tell that to the baddies.' Ryan stood up on the wall and glared at the Little Bother. He stepped forward a little so he could peer down his nose at him and the stones rocked precariously under his feet. 'Come on then,' he said. 'I'll fight you right here. Right now.'

The Little Bother scratched some dirt off a fingernail. 'Don't want to.'

In the apple trees the cicadas had started to chatter.

'Tell you what,' Ryan said. 'If you win I'll join your stupid gang.'

'What if you win?'

Ryan thought about this. 'If I win you won't bother me ever again, and if you're not dead when I've finished, I might not kill you.'

'Not if I kill you first,' the Little Bother said.

He clambered up a mound of rubble beside the wall and stepped gingerly out on to the stones opposite Ryan. They stood facing each other a few feet apart. Slowly Ryan put his arms out, ready to grapple, and the Little Bother, watching him, did the same.

'Come on,' said Ryan. 'Let's see what you've got.'

The Little Bother ran at him fast and with one hand

knocked away his cap and sunglasses.

They wrestled and Ryan took hold of the Little Bother's wrist, twisting the skin until it reddened. The Little Bother cried out, his mouth open and his teeth gappy and uneven, his podgy fists flailing wildly at Ryan's head.

Ryan tried to step aside, but the Little Bother's right knuckles clipped the bridge of his nose and grazed down his front, hitting his breastbone. Caught off balance, he stumbled forward and managed to punch the Little Bother hard in the chest with one well-aimed blow.

The Little Bother steadied himself and turned once more to face Ryan.

They stood on opposite sides of the wall. No longer speaking, just glaring at each other. Their chests rising and falling as they gasped for enough breath to continue the fight.

Suddenly the Little Bother shifted his weight, and tipping back on his feet, dropped his head and ran at Ryan for a third time, aiming to butt him in the stomach. But Ryan was ready and grabbed both his arms. With his right foot, he kicked the Little Bother's shin and, letting go of one arm, clipped him round the side of the head, pinging his ear.

The Little Bother wailed and threw his free hand at Ryan's face, slapping him across the cheek.

'Why don't you stop it?'

'I've stopped it.'

Ryan let go of the Little Bother, who stuck his tongue out at him.

'I won that one,' he said.

Ryan shook his head. 'No, you didn't.'

'Yes I did.'

Ryan would have continued on, but the Little Bother turned to go so he widened his eyes and shouted, 'Don't move! There's a snake!'

'Where?' the Little Bother asked.

'Right there at your feet.'

The Little Bother stood stock still and glanced about, but there was nothing. He turned to Ryan to say something and Ryan shoved him with both hands over the edge of the wall.

The Little Bother teetered for a moment, arms flailing, fingers clutching at the air. Then he fell. The loose stones tumbling in his wake like a miniature avalanche.

Ryan didn't dare look. He just stepped back on to the mound of rubble and scrambled down it. At the bottom he paused and wiped the dirt from his hands. A wave of nausea flooded over him but he pushed it away. He stood and walked aimlessly away a few paces, and then, thinking better of it, turned and hurried round to the other side of the wall.

The Little Bother lay sprawled on the broken stone threshing floor, rocks and gravel strewn around him. His eyes were open but they weren't moving. They just stared blankly at the row of couch grass that sprouted from the cracks in front of his face. A bubble of red blood-spittle frothed from the corner of his mouth as he moaned softly to himself, hiccuping out a series of short noises that fell like lines of dribble to the ground. Ryan's cap and sunglasses lay nearby, so that it looked strangely as if they had fallen from his head.

'Are you OK?' Ryan asked.

The Little Bother shifted slightly and Ryan saw his left arm twisted against his side. The wrist inflamed and swollen, the hand kinked oddly with the fingers splayed out and grasping at the ground.

'I'll go and get help.' Ryan took a few steps back. Stopped, bent over, and slapped the side of his head with a hand. 'Idiot,' he said. 'Idiot. Idiot!'

He knelt down and put a hand on the Little Bother's shoulder.

'Shall I pick you up?' he asked. 'Take you back?' But, except for a low whimper, the Little Bother didn't respond.

Finally, after what seemed like an age, he looked up

at Ryan through a glaze of tears.

'Are you all right?' Ryan asked him again.

The Little Bother spoke through clenched teeth. 'You hurt me, Ryan,' he said. 'You pushed me off the wall.'

'I'm sorry,' Ryan said. 'It was only a game. You will tell them that, won't you? That it was only a game?'

'I don't know.'

'Tell them you fell. It was the stones that did it, not me. I was trying to protect you from the snake. There was a snake on the wall, remember?'

Ryan leaned in close, listening, waiting for an answer.

For a long time the Little Bother stared at him without speaking. Then he lifted his good hand and brushed at a graze on his cheek.

'OK,' he said at last. 'There was a snake on the wall.'

'Good man,' Ryan said. 'You're a good little brother really. Let's get you back to the house.'

He rubbed his sweaty palms on the front of his shorts and slowly reached over and moved the Little Bother's broken arm, placing it down carefully in the centre of his belly. The Little Bother winced as Ryan folded the other hand over it.

'Hold it like that,' Ryan told him and the Little Bother blinked and nodded.

'There. It doesn't look too bad. Now I'm going to pick you up.'

Ryan scooped both his arms under the Little Bother's back and, hugging him close, staggered to his feet.

It had been years since he'd last carried the Little Bother and in that time they'd both got a lot bigger. He leaned against the remaining part of the wall to steady himself, then took a deep breath, and set off up the path.

By the time they'd got halfway to the house the Little Bother had stopped crying and was watching Ryan out of his half closed eyes. 'Did you see me when I fell?' he asked, putting his head on Ryan's shoulder.

Ryan nodded. He could smell the little brother's hair shampoo – the children's one that Mum had brought from England. No More Tears, or whatever it was called.

'I think I was flying a little bit. When I fell off the wall,' his little brother said. 'I was flying in the air for a moment, like Superman. You did see that, didn't you?'

'Of course I did,' Ryan told him.

Carefully he carried his brother up the hill. Past the weeping willow and the water tank, across the brown field and the yard of broken farm implements and up the track to their house, where his parents came running from the front door.

SARKOVSKI'S TOWER
Donald Clark

Sarkovski watched as Laura opened the little package wrapped in pink paper. She took out a necklace of turquoise glass beads set in silver plated leaves. She walked over to the mirror and fastened it around her neck and looked at herself, half turning to left and right so that the overhead light flashed on the beads. She was dressed in her work shoes, solid, low heeled, scuffed at the toes. Sarkovski thought she should have on the white high heels she loved to wear when they went out Saturday nights to the pub or the pictures. She was still wearing her work clothes too, which was strange because she must have been back for quite a while, as he was late home himself. A thick purple cardigan covered the regulation white blouse and black skirt that all the girls, of whatever age, had to wear behind the counter in the department store. He was surprised too that her face did not light up with the present, the way it normally did whenever he gave her something or whenever she saw something she liked.

When her face lit up, he could actually feel the glow. Her mouth would open wide and he could see her little white teeth, and her eyes sparkling, and for an instant she would be like a child who has seen a decorated Christmas tree for the first time. This time though, her face was serious. Viewed from the side, her nose, which normally appeared short and slightly turned up, today looked long, and her upper lip was drawn down over the lower. Her forehead, tilted forward, made her chin squeeze against her neck. She seemed older. Laura stopped looking in the mirror, her eyes were downcast, her gaze fixed several inches in front of her breast.

What made him turn his own head then? He looked round the room and saw parked behind the door a brown plastic suitcase with a leather strap buckled round it and a two-wheeled shopping trolley with a tartan pannier. He turned back to look at her, his eyes now as large as an owl's, the corners of his mouth sagging as if suddenly feeling the weight of all his years. His mouth opened but he said nothing.

'Oh, Jan, Jan,' she said, 'I saw my mum today and she said to me where are you living now? And I told her I was staying with you and she said I was a dirty filthy girl. And I said I wasn't because you are a lovely man and I was going to marry you. And she just laughed and said I was daft as well as dirty and that you are as old as my dad. And, Jan Jan, it's true, isn't it, you are old? I mean not really old, but older than me and you are going to die, aren't you? Then where will I be, Jan Jan? I've always loved you, Janny Jan Jan, but I'm scared and I don't want to be on my own and I will be and you won't be able to do anything about it because you will be dead and even if you're not dead I will have to look after you and my mum as well and I don't want that because I want to live.'

How could he tell her that he too wanted to live? That he'd been living all the time he was with her and that he wouldn't die and that she might die before him, and that he had seen so many dead people it didn't matter because people died anyway but you could always go on living. But he no longer believed that. In an instant he felt the death he'd evaded for so many years. Felt a wave of sorrows rise up ready to overwhelm his defences, to drown him. All strength was gone. He remembered as a child seeing the river burst its banks and a dead cow floating in the swirling waters, four rigid legs sticking in the air.

'But where will you go, Lo Lo?' he asked.

'Oh, don't worry, Jan Jan,' she said. 'I've got a friend who will rent me a room. But you mustn't call me Lo Lo because I'm not Lo Lo any more. I am very sorry, Jan Jan, because you know I love you, you'll always be the only one for me and I don't mind at all that you're a Catholic and I don't care what my mum says. Do you want the necklace back?'

'No, Lo Lo, I mean –' and he became confused, he didn't know what to call her, to call her Laura now would mean the end. 'No, you keep it, I buy it for you only,' he said.

Now her face lit up, the smile that he thought was for him alone. She rushed over and put her arms round his neck, but she would not let him kiss her on the lips. 'I am not Lo Lo any more.'

'I will help you with your bag?' He said it as a question. So suddenly had he been disenfranchised that he dare not assume a gesture of friendship would be accepted.

'No, Jan Jan, you stay here. I will be all right. Please stay here and don't follow me or look out of the window or anything. I will write to you as soon as I get settled in, to see that you are all right.'

He did as she asked and sat on his old sofa as she carried the suitcase out through the front door, dragging the trolley behind her. He did not get up from the sofa to look out of the window and so did not see a young man, about her age, take her bag and load it into the boot of his car.

He sat there for an hour or maybe longer, and then, when he

was sure she was not going to come back that night, he went into his garden and started to dig a hole.

That was the start of the Tower: a hole. He did not have any plan for the Tower, or for the hole. He just knew that he had to dig and keep digging until he was exhausted. As he dug a soft rain fell. The rain mixed with the sweat on his brow and rolled down, stinging his eyes and collecting in the crevices of his face. Then the drops rolled to the end of his chin and dripped into the hole as he bent his head forward to push down on the spade. That first night he dug down to the depth of his shovel handle, and fashioned a rectangle five feet by three feet. It had the makings of a grave, a shallow resting place where he could curl up and be forgotten. He went inside and got his raincoat and a cushion from the sofa. He put the cushion at the bottom of the hole, climbed in and lay down with his head resting on it. He lay on his back with his knees drawn up and the coat draped over him. It had stopped raining now and the clouds started to clear away. It was early autumn and the air had been warm, but now it began to chill. Sarkovski did not notice. He rested one arm behind his head and smoked cigarettes and thought about Laura. He could imagine her now with her lovely golden hair: she might be crying and missing him, and he wanted to go and find her. He knew he must not do that; he tried to think of other things instead. He remembered the time they had taken the train and spent the day at the seaside. They had paddled in the sea and eaten fish and chips and candyfloss and drunk lager and smoked and he had had a nap on the beach. When they walked hand in hand along the front past the pier and the bingo hall, they had been oblivious to the looks from people trying to figure out the relationship between this middle-aged man and the girl who looked half his age. She looked so young that in the pub the barmaid had almost refused to serve her, even though she was nearly thirty. That hadn't been so long ago, not really, and now it was gone and he didn't understand where.

***

He slept for a few hours and then in the early morning woke up and smoked and thought strange, disconnected thoughts about her. He was cold and stiff. He climbed out of the hole and went off to work in the plastics factory. That day he stood by his injection moulding machine, making translucent food containers in various colours. These were a new line and the firm was doing well out of them. Nobody came to talk to him and at tea break and lunchtime he sat in the yard and smoked.

In the evening he went home. He checked to see if there was any sign of Laura having been there. There was none. She had left some clothes in the wardrobe and they were still hanging there. He found other things: a hairband in the chest of drawers, a nail file in the medicine cabinet, an old magazine under the bed. When he saw each of these, Sarkovski turned away. He wanted to go round and stand outside her mother's house and wait for her, just to get a glimpse, just to see her. What harm could it do if he stood over the road in the bus shelter and just looked? No, he wasn't going to do that.

He picked up the magazine and laid it on the bed and then lay down next to it. It was a style magazine for teenagers and young women, full of advice on how to find a partner, how to tell if your best friend was seeing your husband and who was hot in the entertainment world. The contents meant nothing to Sarkovski but the feel of it, the smell of it, reminded him of her. She used to lie in bed reading it and telling him about pop stars and the clothes she was going to buy and the way she was going to have her hair done, and then she would put the light out and cuddle him.

He lay in the deepening gloom until the last of the September light had gone. Now it was completely dark in the flat. He had felt sure she would come back and say it was all a mistake and she just wanted to get into bed with him and read her magazine.

But she didn't come that night or the next night or the one after that. In the days that followed Sarkovski went to work in the plastics factory and turned out countless food containers that would be used by happy families. It was him who did all this, but it didn't feel like him. When he looked down at his hands they seemed to be detached, removed from the being trapped inside his head. In his mind he called out her name. He was standing on a cliff calling out across an empty sea, ' Lo Lo, Lo Lo,' and he had conversations with her as she held his hand and told him she loved him.

Then one night, at the end of the working week, he came home and there was still no message from her. He went into the garden and looked at the hole he'd started to dig the night that Laura went away. He climbed into the hole and he dug. After maybe three hours of resolute work he stopped and surveyed what he had done. The hole was now five feet deep and eight feet square, with mounds of earth and rubble around the edges. He had dug up rusted tin cans, half-bricks, a rotted gas mask, part of a window frame. He inadvertently sliced through a worm and apologized to it. He had broken his nails and grazed his fingers, but as he lit a cigarette he felt warm for the first time in five days. He had laboured on building sites and knew what had to be done to make this into a real hole, a hole that anyone could be proud of. He cut toe holds into the wall of the hole, heaved himself out and went to the corner of the garden, to an old shed that had collapsed before he'd moved into his flat. A few of the timbers were still sound and he pulled them free. He whacked some vertically into the hole against the edges to act as supports and pushed others horizontally behind the uprights. The framework would stop the sides collapsing, the greatest fear for any hole digger. Then he brought out the stepladder he kept behind the kitchen door and placed that in the hole and climbed down. That night he dug another three feet. It was a taxing job to throw the earth up on to the edges and tricky to climb out.

Foyles Bookshop
Royal Festival Hall
London SE1 8XX

Tel: 020 7437 5660
www.foyles.co.uk
Open Monday to Sunday 10:00 - 22:00

TEL NO: 020 7437 5660
VAT NO: 238 7867 10

23 10 14 19:09   SALE 27 8568 CLAIRESJP

PRODUCT	QTY	VAT

Tales From The Blue Room
9780957191615   1   6.99 Z

ZERO RATE	6.99	6.99
TOTAL	1	6.99
CASH		7.00
TOTAL TENDERED		7.00
CHANGE		0.01

****
** FOYLES LOYALTY CARD IS AVAILABLE **
If you had a loyalty card, the number of
points earned by this sale would be 27
If you take out a new loyalty card, these
points can be added retrospectively.
****

Except for 2nd hand goods printed music
eReaders Giftcards and unsealed CDs DVDs
goods in resaleable condition may be
returned or exchanged at any branch with
valid receipt within 14 days of purchase
Your statutory rights are not affected

Over the next week or so his life took on a routine: he woke up thinking about her, then he got ready for work, went to the plastics factory and extruded food containers, came home and his life began. He checked to see if she had written a letter or pushed a note through the letter box and when he saw that she had not he started work.

By now the hole extended so that it covered all the area that had once, long ago, been a lawn. That was when the house had been a bourgeois villa, full of tinkling laughter and summer frocks, before it was broken up into mean one-bedroom flats like the one he and Lo Lo had shared. It had been their little kingdom, with her as a princess and him as the smiling lord.

Every night after digging he lay on the bed and read her magazine and smoked. Then, when it was late, he would roam the streets looking for materials to shore up the hole. Old doors and drainpipes from skips, timber from building sites, dustbins and garden gates. He built a series of ramps and platforms so that he could move in and out freely, and then he stretched a tarpaulin over it so that he could work when it was raining. He put a Primus stove in there to make tea and an old rocking chair he found on a street corner. This was more home to him now than the flat and he thought he might move in permanently once he had finished digging; only he had no idea when that would be.

In all this time nobody, not one person, asked him what he was doing. At work he was an outcast shadowing the herd, limping behind. Then one night, as he was emerging from the hole with a hurricane lamp, a man in the flat above his, pushed up the sash window and leaned out.

'What yer building there?' he said.

Sarkovski looked up at him, the glow from the lamp lighting the underside of his face. The shock of the question stunned him.

'It's a hole,' was all he could say.

'What for?' asked the man.

Now he really didn't know what to say. He looked up at his interrogator, his eyes pleading that he be asked no more.

'She's gone,' he said, finally.

'Well, yer'll never get her back that way, yer daft bugger.'

The man at the window tipped back a can of lager, swallowed its contents and tossed it into the garden next door. He had done this many times before and there was now a colony of indestructible aluminium cans gleaming in the grass.

'Yer've just gotta forget her.'

The man turned away from the window. Sarkovski could hear laughter coming from inside.

It was true. He was never going to get her back that way. What had he been thinking? All that digging and she hadn't even noticed or cared. He thought now that she didn't care, maybe she never had done, all that time they'd been together. But no, he couldn't believe that. He knew that she loved him, and all the things that she'd said were true, when she laughed and winked at him and called him 'Jan Jan, my lord', and he kissed the little crescent-shaped scar on her forehead which she had got falling off her tricycle when she was six years old. He climbed back into the hole and squatted in one corner. He spent maybe two hours there, anyway enough to smoke five or ten cigarettes, the extinguished butts pressed by his thumb into the mud as if they might germinate. That was the darkest night. But it wasn't as he had imagined the end would feel. There was no searing pain, no crushing realization, no hubbub of voices mocking him, just this: a bird of summer crippled and bowing its head in the autumn knowing it has nowhere to go and will not survive the winter.

He stood up and paced around the hole. If he walked the length and breadth of it, like it was a big earthy prison cell, and if he did that perhaps half a million times, he might have walked as far as China, or as far as Poland, where he came from. But he didn't do that: instead he took three gravel boards he had scavenged from an old fence and nailed the ends together to form a free-standing pyramid. That was the thing about the place where he lived: you could do all that during the night, banging and bashing, and nobody gave a damn, and even if they did you could ignore them. People could shout and scream and beat each other and throw cans out of the window and it was nobody else's business. It was a patchwork world of a thousand private anarchies which sometimes overlapped or collided but which never interlocked. Each had its own lodestar and compass, and each came to its own separate end. The pyramid stood in the bottom of the hole, pointing the way to the stars, and it seemed to Sarkovski that it was pointing to somewhere else that he had never been, somewhere he should try.

That night he went out and roamed far and wide. He paced like a wolf along deserted streets, his head turning from side to side as he hunted, his eyes and the saliva on his tongue sparkling in the street lights. He found what he was looking for: the materials to build a new dream that would rise up from his garden and look heaven in the eye.

Again and again he went out and came back with more scaffolding poles, beams, purlins and floorboards. He took a bucketful of steel clamps from one building site where the scaffolding had been half completed and lugged back an eight-foot-long oak beam, six inches square, from an abandoned grocery shop whose roof was falling in. The next evening after work he came home and started to build. At first he had no idea what it should look like, then he saw a kind of pattern: scaffolding poles knocked vertically into the earth at each corner and then, at intervals in between, horizontals fixed with putlocks and a platform laid across with old floorboards. By the end of that evening he had built enough for it to rise just above the surface of the hole. Over the next few evenings he added on to it so that now it reached ten or fifteen feet above the ground.

One night the man upstairs opened the window and said, 'What yer building?'

'It's my dream,' said Sarkovski.

'Yeah?' said the man. 'Want a beer?'

He threw a can down to Sarkovski. It fizzed and frothed and spurted over his face when he pulled the ring to open it. The cold sticky liquid dribbled down his chin and neck and then on to his chest. He drank the remainder in one gulp. It warmed him and talked to him like a friend. For the first time in weeks, he felt like himself.

'Very good. Thank you,' he said.

The man pulled his head back in and closed the window.

The construction took place each night and within a fortnight it reached as high as an old apple tree in the next-door garden. Each morning another five or six feet had been added to it. Sarkovski now had to go ever further to get the materials. Early one morning, standing on a platform made of an old bedroom door with faux panelling, Sarkovski got the impression that he was standing on the bridge of a ship, that he was the captain guiding the destiny of his vessel. By the moonlight he could now look out across the gardens of the dilapidated Victorian houses that made up his neighbourhood. He stood gripping the railing as a wet October wind, like clammy fingers, ran through his hair. The pain of Laura was almost forgotten. She was now a face tossing on the ocean below; then the face howled and he knew he had not yet reached harbour.

During all this time he got by on maybe two or three hours of sleep a night. He had never known such energy, such strength. Never once did he miss work or even arrive late. He was always freshly shaved with a clean shirt and he went to his machine and turned out multicoloured food containers.

It was when the Tower reached the level of the third storey of the house that people began to take notice. At night he ran a cable out from his flat and hung lamps on it so that he could carry on working. A tarpaulin tied to the top of it protected him from rain. The week before Christmas he had reached five feet above the roof level. Using wire cutters, he snipped away at a metal dustbin lid and fashioned a star which he fixed to the top of his Tower. People went out of their way to come and see. Two days before Christmas there was a traffic jam in Inkerman Street, where he lived, and the police were called. The next day two men from the council came. One of them, a black man dressed in a dark suit, took the lead. He explained that he and his colleague, a short, plump wheezing white man, were from the Environmental Health Department and they were investigating reports of an unauthorized construction. They could see the Tower plainly from the street, silhouetted against the grey December sky. Overnight Sarkovski had hung red glowing paraffin lamps which he'd found on a building site. He had added a small advertising hoarding and a teddy bear.

'I'm afraid, sir, that if you don't have planning permission for your building, and you do not appear to have planning permission, you will be required to remove the construction completely, at your own expense. Otherwise you will face the probability of heavy fines and claims for costs. If you want our advice, sir, you will need to make a proper application, completed by an authorized and qualified professional. But frankly, sir, we don't believe it will meet with council policy.' And did they add this? Did they say, 'And another word of advice, sir, this is not going to bring her back either'? But Sarkovski was not sure, because he didn't understand what they were saying. He knew nothing about planning permission or the correct way of going about things. Anyway, the men disappeared, and it being the age they all lived in, they did not say, 'Merry Christmas.'

He carried on building and by the end of the holiday he had added another storey. Now it occurred to him that it needed balconies so that he could look out north, south, east and west. He would be able to put his hand to his forehead and shield his eyes and scan the horizon. One balcony was built from an old pallet. Another was made up from an avocado-coloured plastic bath. He used a shopping trolley for the third and for the last one, facing north, he built a platform from pine floorboards.

All this time he worked at the plastics factory. Now he was moulding toilet seats, which, through a patented technique, could have objects such as imitation starfish or coins moulded into a transparent body. One version had a musical box that played when the lid was raised. One night he came home and there was a folded note pushed under the door. It said, 'Am I Lo Lo, am I?' That was the night that he worked until four in the morning and put the finishing touches to a turret built from copper piping and roofed with beer cans beaten flat and nailed to pieces of curved plywood. In the moonlight they glittered like fish scales.

By now he was famous. A reporter from the local paper came to interview Sarkovski about his strange construction, but couldn't tell from his answers why he was building it, so the reporter supplied his own explanation. It was, it seemed, to honour the idea that an Englishman's home was his castle. Beneath the headline: 'Polish Prince Builds Castle In The Air,' the reporter ran his article. It told how in England refugees could come from any part of the world and build their dreams. The newspaper had been running a campaign against the local authority's planning policy and so when the council said it would be seeking a court order to remove the Tower the paper was able to thunder about 'hard-hearted bureaucracy', although it was careful not to say it was in favour of unauthorized construction. It was enough that David should be pitted against Goliath; who won the contest was unimportant.

It was a spectacle. People came and donated planks, ironing boards, nails and screws; a welder turned up to melt rolled-steel joists together and a carpenter offered to build a porch entrance with a cruck roof. By April the Tower was half as high as Nelson's Column. When the council announced that it was going to employ contractors to pull it down, there was a demonstration outside the Town Hall which then moved on to Inkerman Street. But Sarkovski was unaware of this. He did not notice the crowds gathered in the street below, the hot dog vendors, and the beer stall set up by his neighbour. He did not hear the buzzing motor of an airship hired by a French camera crew or the chanting of 'Let Him Be', sung to the Beatles tune. He did not see the placards proclaiming 'Tower Power' which were waved up high. He did not smell the burning rubber as cars were overturned and set alight.

On this day of deconstruction Sarkovski was above all this, above pushing crowds and violent passions. He was in the tallest turret, which he had finished the night before. He had hung red satin curtains gifted by an old lady who lived around the corner in Balaclava Mansions. Looking out across the town, with the curtains flapping in the wind, he could see hills and fields beyond. He could not see Laura, not yet. As the demolition men started their task, he rocked from side to side and wondered how long it would take to build one more storey.

COSMO AND DAMIAN'S CHRISTMAS OUTING
Paul Yates

'It's not exactly luxury,' Damian said, as they boarded the train at Paddington, 'but there's something romantic about going to sleep on a train and waking up somewhere else. I've always loved it.'

'I did Austerlitz–Madrid once, through the snowy high sierras,' Cos said. 'Feels like being in a movie.'

'It'll give us a liminal zone before the festivities,' Damian said. 'Have you got the bottle of red?'

'That's nice. I'm feeling a bit liminal myself – it's been a beast of a term, too much melancholy – and, yes, in my bag with some pretzels and it's a screw top.'

'I thought melancholy was good for English majors?'

The couchette was a wonder of mechanical miniaturization. The bunks were folded into the wall and two comfortable armchairs faced the engine.

'Put the luggage up top, with the spare pillows,' Damian said.

'This is so cute,' Cos said, opening the narrow wooden door

to the wet room. 'I don't know how people share these things with strangers – I'd be terrified of farting.'

'Let's have some music,' Damian said, fishing in his bag for the miniature speaker. 'How about the lovely Bach cantata, *Auf* thingy? It'll get us in the mood for an English Christmas.'

'Let joy be unconfined,' Cos said.

They shared the bottle of wine, drinking from the plastic tooth glasses, as the train lurched towards the west. After an edible but uninspiring dinner they tumbled back to the couchette, where, now, the bunks were down and small chocolates had been left on the pillows.

'The choc fairy's been,' Cos said.

'We must tip the attendant when we get off for this magical transformation,' Damian said, 'even though it only takes thirty seconds and he doesn't have any passports to deal with as Cornwall is yet to become independent.'

Cos undid the top button of Damian's jeans and kissed him.

'Let's do stone, paper, scissors for the top bunk,' he said.

Cos got the top bunk.

Sitting with legs dangling, Cos listened to the shriek of the gulls and the sounds of Damian, about half a metre away, in the wet room. If he took much longer there would be no time for a shower before breakfast, something he felt he needed. The night had seemed to last forever as he drifted in and out of sleep, gently tugged this way and that by the movement of the train and the eeriness of moments when it stopped for no apparent reason. The coffee and croissant proved surprisingly good and Cos willingly parted with a fiver as the smart attendant, waiting on the platform, hoped they had enjoyed their journey, looked forward to seeing them again soon and wished them a merry Christmas.

'There's Dad.'

Damian waved as a tall man with Damian's soft oval face and

black wavy hair came towards them, hands lifted in welcome. He wore a Barbour and green wellingtons and hugged Damian, slapping him on the back.

'Lovely to see you, Dami, and great to meet you, Cosmo,' he said, turning to Cos, pumping his hand and gripping his forearm.

'It's great to be here, Mr Lutyens,' Cos said. 'Thanks for inviting me.'

'It's Oliver and, you're very welcome,' he said, momentarily intensifying his grip. 'Wagon's just outside. Both had a good term, I hope. How was the journey?'

Out in the country the air was keen with a harsh winter light. Turning off the main road, the ancient Land Rover bumped its way through narrow lanes with high hedgerows. After a few kilometres they came to a rise where they could see the cliffs and the sea before them. Passing through a small hamlet, they followed a potholed cinder track and drove through a pair of dilapidated gates with hinges red with salty rust.

'The estate,' Damian said, 'all two hectares of it.'

On either side of the drive was blackened gorse and marsh grass singing in the wind. About half a kilometre away below them they could see the house, perched on a promontory that jutted out from the cliff.

Oliver stopped on the crest of the hill.

'Looks so romantic and mysterious from here. I forget until someone with new eyes comes,' he said, turning to grin at Cos, who sat on a bench in the back, surrounded by the paraphernalia of a country vet.

They rolled forward into a dip and the house disappeared, to rise up before them as the path veered suddenly downwards along the edge of the cliff. They came to rest on a windy plateau with the sea crashing noisily beneath them.

The house stood between the small plateau and the sea. Jagged coastline reached into the mist to the east and the west. Oliver parked in the lee of a rock face into which garages and an outhouse had been built. Cos and Damian got out and stood, taking in the scene.

'What a great place,' Cos said, 'every bit as amazing as you described it. So high up, and rugged and rocky, and not another sign of humanity anywhere. It doesn't feel like England at all.'

The building was large, old, made of granite and oddly shaped. Built into the rock, the entrance was on the first floor. It was decidedly vernacular. The soft curves of the various roofs gave it an art nouveau look. To the front and sides were large windows with thick stone frames and mullions that looked ecclesiastical. A heavy, ugly turret with a Norman cap looked out of place on one corner.

'I was born here,' Damian said, as they went into the dark hall. 'I wasn't supposed to be, but my mother said she was taken by surprise. Luckily Dad was around – it's pretty much the same as sheep. Mind those steps. They're a bit deceptive and there's not much light.'

Cos stumbled behind Damian down the few wide, curving wooden treads to a landing lit by a glass door looking out to sea. The kitchen was large, warm and untidy. In one corner the wind whistled in the chimney of a blue Aga.

'Let's have some coffee with Dad and then I'll take you exploring before the light goes. I want to show you my favourite place in the world. You can see it from the window.'

'Sounds good to me,' Cos said.

He slipped his arms round Damian as he filled the kettle, kissing his hair and nuzzling his nape.

'Careful,' Damian said. 'We haven't told him yet.'

'But we are going to, aren't we?' Cos said. 'I can't believe he hasn't guessed. You're nearly twenty and, in the right light, as camp as Agincourt. Do you think you should tell him tonight at supper? I'll hold your hand.'

'I'll think about it.'

'Well done,' Oliver said, padding into the kitchen in thick, marled socks. 'You make the coffee and I'll find some madeleines. They should be à point by now – we can always dunk them if they're a bit dry. I've taken your bags up. You're in your old room at the top of the house, Dami, and Cos is next door in the turret. The heating is on and you should be quite comfy.'

'Sounds lovely, Dad, thanks. How's the practice going?' Damian asked, as he pushed down the plunger on a grubby cafetière.

'It's fine. Pays the rent, though more farmers are thinking twice about staying in dairy nowadays. Still, I've got some sick cows to visit this afternoon – they don't know it's Christmas Eve.'

'What about the skeleton, Dad? I was telling Cos about it earlier.'

'Bloody nuisance,' Oliver said, he turned to Cos. 'Builders found it, excavating for the new garage, and, quite rightly I guess, all human remains have to be investigated by the coroner. They thought it might be medieval at first, as there were traces of it being wrapped in a bluish cloak. Finally, it seems it was a teenage female, died probably in the eighteenth century, before this house, although there was one on the site. Unsurprisingly, there's no contemporary evidence of a missing girl and no explanation of how she ended up in what must have been a very remote spot.'

'That's spooky,' Damian said. 'I spent my whole childhood playing on her grave.'

'Did she die naturally?' Cos asked.

'Impossible to say,' Oliver replied. 'There was no indication of cause of death and the skeleton wasn't complete. Foxes tend to dig up shallow graves. The bones get interred somewhere, I think. That's it, and now I must go. There's a couple of pheasants for supper. I'll pop them in the Aga on my way out. Back about six.'

* * *

Cos went up to get his pea coat and scarf while Damian found him some wellingtons. The room was at the top of the turret with long views of the sea and the coastline. Cos looked down to a deep cove cut into the cliff, just below the house, where a figure in blue stood on the strand line, looking out to sea. It was hard to see what sex the person was. Cos shivered involuntarily.

They climbed the drive for a couple of hundred metres before turning off along a narrow track that wound round the top of the cliff before descending towards the sea. The day had become colder, with ominous purple clouds beginning to mass in the north-west.

'Come on, Cos. We've only got an hour or so before the light goes.'

'I'm not used to this sort of thing, you know,' Cos said, stumbling over some briar roots. 'You don't get much of this terrain in Dulwich. I'll want a donkey and a guide if we have to go much further.'

They reached a sheltered plateau. Damian sat on a rock waiting for Cos. Before them the dark outline of a ruined machine house, from an old mine, rose above the skyline.

'How ridiculously Gothic,' Cos said.

The path now zigzagged downward, sometimes centimetres away from the cliff edge, until they came to a narrow cleft that curved away into the towering rock. Cos peered into the blackness.

'Watch out,' Damian said. 'There are some sudden drops along this stretch.'

The path ended abruptly on a ledge. The dripping, dark silence changed to the salt wind and light, and the sound of the breakers and the calling of seabirds. They had to scramble over massive boulders and negotiate some slimy outcrops of rocks before reaching the fine sand of the cove floor. Behind them were deep triangles of caves running back into the cliff. Faces of shining rock ran with water, leaving long streaks of rust red washed from the ore. A waterfall fed a rivulet that coursed through the sand to mingle with the sea. Flat rocks with deep black pools lined the sides of the cove. The back of the cove was littered with multicoloured boulders the size of small cars.

Damian held up his arms and twirled around laughing.

'It's lovely to be back here, and even better to be sharing it with you.'

He hugged Cos tightly.

'Isn't it wonderful? We've got it all to ourselves. Get your boots off – we're going paddling.'

'But how will we dry our feet and get the sand out from between our toes, and won't we get frostbite?'

'Don't be such a poof.'

Cos looked on as Damian pulled off his boots and socks.

'All right, I'll do it, as long as you recognize it as the supreme self-sacrifice.'

'I'd expect no less from you. Put your wellies up on that rock with mine.' Damian pulled his jeans up to his knees and ran towards the surf. 'Come on.'

They stood together, holding up their jeans as the clear, freezing water lapped around their shins.

'Greater love hath no man,' Cos said.

'If it looks like there's a big wave coming, leg it up the beach or you'll get drenched.'

They dried their feet as best they could and walked up the sloping sand to explore the caves.

'It must be an illusion,' Cos said, 'but the opening we came into the cove by has disappeared, there's just solid rock.'

'I know. I guess it's because it's narrow and no light gets through. It only appears when you're level with it, but don't worry, I know exactly where it is.'

They climbed over the boulders and went into the deepest of the caves. Dripping water echoed around them and their voices were amplified. Cos looked down towards the sea, which was now coming in, with the curved white lines of foam stretching towards them. That must have been where the blue figure stood, just staring out to sea.

'Do people come here much?'

'Nutty anglers and the occasional dog walker mostly. A few intrepid families in the summer. When mum was still with us we'd trek down and barbie, fish and sausages and lovely Texas toast.'

Cos pulled Damian towards him and kissed him on the lips.

'Let's go,' he said. 'It's starting to rain and there's still a couple of hours before your dad gets back.'

'Right. We'll have to get out before the tide in any case. Come on – last one into bed's a sissy.'

The house door closed behind them. Cos turned to Damian, undid his jacket and slid his hands around his waist. He moved them slowly up his back, feeling the slight play of muscles as Damian moved against him. He squeezed Damian and pulled him tightly against his own body, breathing in the scent of salty warmth from his skin. Lips, cooled by the sea air, pressed gently against the softness of Damian's neck. Cos pushed his hands into the back pockets of Damian's jeans and drew them tightly together so each could feel the other's hardness. Cos's lips stopped to brush against Damian's ear before briefly touching, with great gentleness, lips that showed almost grey in the oval of Damian's face. Cos kissed each side of his mouth and put the tip of his tongue into the corner, but not as far as his teeth. He kissed his forehead, his closed eyes and the tip and sides of his nose. His arms moved again to encircle Damian's back as he kissed the soft upper planes of his cheeks and the entrancing roughness of his chin. Cos held Damian's head between his two hands and kissed him on the mouth. Moving his head to the side, he kissed him again and felt his mouth open for him.

* * *

'Dami, can you and Cosmo lay the small table in the dining room and open some wine? I'm gasping. There's some Pouilly in the fridge. Dinner in twenty minutes.'

'Sure thing, Dad – delish.'

A large round mahogany table, set in front of an ornate fireplace, dominated the dining room. Behind it was a dark oak sideboard. In the bay window an old kitchen table served most occasions. Cos stood by the window, looking down through the rain at the dark shapes of the cove, listening to the crashing waves.

'The storm's passed. The lightning was magnificent. Can I see a blue light flickering down there? Look – on the far side of the cove.'

'It'll be an angler,' Damian said, peering into the dark. 'I told you they were bonkers. They risk life and limb when that tide comes in. Perhaps he wants some sea bass for Christmas dinner.'

Their shoulders touched as they stood together, sipping wine, looking into the night.

'Are you up for it?' Cos asked.

'I don't think I can do it right now. Don't be cross – I do love you,' Damian said. He stroked Cos's arm. 'It was easier for you with your metrosexual parents. Your dad seems to have known before you did.'

'Such astonishing prescience,' Cos said, and smiled. 'Promise me you'll tell him before we're forty.' He kissed his finger and laid it on Damian's lips.

Damian poured them some more wine.

'I'll see if Dad wants another,' he said, and took the bottle into the kitchen.

Cos stared out at the dark cove, emptying his glass without noticing.

Oliver came in with a cast-iron casserole and put it on the table. He took off the lid and fragrant steam filled the air.

'That smells great,' Cos said.

'I'll just get the potatoes out of the bottom oven and we're set,' Oliver said, disappearing back into the kitchen.

Oliver returned and sat down. He raised his glass.

'Cheers, guys. It's great to have you around. It gets lonely. Here's to an outbreak of animal health for at least a few days.'

Damian put the coffee tray down on the occasional table beside the fire in the sitting room. He handed rounds cups and glasses of brandy, before joining Cos on one of the couches that flanked the hearth. The large room had two bays, obscured by heavy curtains against the wind, and was mostly in darkness. Standard lamps lit the area around the fire. Oliver sat with his feet up on the low padded fender.

For a while the three of them were quiet, eyes drawn by the flickering light. Oliver got up and kicked the logs to produce some flame before throwing a couple more on.

'What are you getting up to during the vac?' he asked.

'We'd like to stay here and chill for a while, Dad, if that's OK with you. We've got essays to write. Then London, and see Cos's folks on the way back to Brighton.'

'I'd love to do some more exploring,' Cos said. 'I've never really seen the rugged bits of Cornwall.'

'You've already seen Trefillick cove,' Damian said, putting his hand on Cos's arm. 'That's the best bit for miles.'

'That's true,' Oliver said, 'and rambling around there, looking for pirates' treasure and smugglers' caves was how Dami spent most of his days.'

'You helped,' Damian said.

'Yes, I did. After we lost your mother, I'm afraid I got a bit possessive and I preferred you being in view, especially down at the cove. I couldn't have kept you out of it even if I had wanted to.'

'You were great, Dad, although we never found a single

dubloon, did we? I know it looks dangerous down there, but I made it into a secure world. I could even see the house.'

Oliver swirled his brandy and lifted his glass.

'Absent friends,' he said.

He stood up and put his tumbler on the tray.

'And now I'll say goodnight – I have to get up and cook the goose tomorrow.'

'It's my favourite meal of the year. We'll help, won't we, Cos? He's very well house-trained, Dad.'

'We'd love to, and we'll wash up before we go to bed.'

'Steady on,' Damian said.

When Oliver had gone Cos leaned over and kissed Damian.

'I'm not going to push you at all,' Cos said, 'but we did say that if we did it at Christmas, which is kind of outside ordinary time, good cheer and all that, it would be easier for everyone, and so I suggest breakfast tomorrow. I'll do the talking if you like. But if you don't want to we'll drop it for now – I don't want it ruining our break.'

'Fine, we'll do it,' Damian said, putting his arms round Cos and laying his head on his shoulder. 'Tell me you love me.'

'Dearest Damian, or may I call you Dami? I could not love you more. Truly, you are the world to me.'

Cos sat in a chair reading by the light of his beside lamp. Apart from the now soughing wind, the only sound was what he supposed were mice, scampering to and fro in the roof space at the top of the turret. Sleep eluded him, as it so often did. He got up, drew the curtains and looked out at the moon casting an endlessly shifting cone of light on the surface of the sea, tapering to the horizon. Above the horizon so many stars were visible that the vault looked almost solid. Light bleached the landscape into a faded monochrome. Looking down at the cove, he saw the blue figure standing in the surf. As he watched, it turned its face towards the house. He went and sat down. What on earth was this creature? Had he conjured it? Cos checked his watch. It was three o'clock. Pulling on jeans and a jumper, and with his shoes in his hand, he went quietly down to the front door. Leaving it on the latch, he walked swiftly up the steep drive to the path that he and Damian had taken earlier. He could hear his feet crunch on the cinders and the wind softly swishing the marsh grass.

Moon shadows obscured the ground and Cos tripped several times, once falling forward on to a jagged rock, ripping his jeans and cutting his leg. At the plateau the old machine house loomed, glowing in the sea mist. Cos stopped to get his breath, leaning forward, hands on his knees. *Why do I imagine it will disappear if I don't hurry?* Treading more carefully along the precipitous zigzag track, he entered the near-total darkness of the cleft, feeling his way carefully forward with his feet to avoid the sudden drops in the uneven descent. Touching the rock walls as he went forward, he sensed, rather than saw, the curve that told him the end of the track was near. The eerie light began to soften the wall to his left and then he was on the ledge above the cove, with the sound of the surf and the wind tugging at him. The bright silvery light bouncing off the sea was startling and it took some moments for his eyes to become accustomed. At first he saw nothing, but then the figure was before him, not a hundred metres away. A blue tunic moved in the wind and light bleached hair fell on to thin shoulders. The figure turned slowly to face Cos, its face hidden in shadow. A hand was raised, palm towards him, in greeting or beckoning he did not know. He stepped forward.

On Christmas morning, a strong south-westerly blew flurries of snow around the house and dashed the breakers on to the rocks below. Damian, yawning and stretching, padded across the cold wooden floorboards to Cos's room. Cos was not there. The bedside light was on, but then the sun had barely risen. Damian showered and was mildly surprised that Cos hadn't appeared. Dressed, he went downstairs. Oliver was in the kitchen, making stuffing for the goose. Damian went over and kissed him.

'Merry Christmas, Dad. Where's Cos?'

'I haven't seen him. I thought the pair of you were upstairs.'

Damian checked the dining and sitting rooms, and called Cos's name up the stairs, to no effect.

'Perhaps he's taking the air?' Oliver said.

'It's barely light, he doesn't know his way around and there's a gale blowing. I'll check round the grounds.'

Damian got his coat from the hall, where Cos's still hung. He went out, calling Cos's name and raking a landscape that constantly shifted with the moving clouds of snow. His voice disappeared into the howl of the wind and the hissing of the grass. Damian shivered and rushed back into the house, banging the door. He tumbled down the stairs into the kitchen.

'I can't see him, Dad. The door was on the latch but his coat is still here... What's happened? Where's he got to?'

'I've been up since seven and it's nearly half eight. If he did go for a walk he could easily have got lost on the cliff paths.'

'He does get up in the night sometimes, when he can't sleep – he may have gone out.'

'You really do know each other well, don't you?' Oliver said.

'Dad, we've got to find him! He may have fallen – or anything,' Damian said. He dashed tears from his cheeks. 'I feel sick.'

'You'll be fine, Dami,' Oliver said, 'but you're right, it's bloody cold out there. We'd better check the house thoroughly first – you do that and I'll gather the necessaries together.'

When Damian got back to the hall, Oliver had assembled rope, binoculars, first aid and a flask of brandy. He stuffed an insulating blanket into a rucksack and threw it to Damian.

'Get above the garages and scan what you can before we go,' Oliver said, handing Damian the binoculars. 'Where did you say you went yesterday?'

'The cove.'

'Then we should check that out before we worry the coastguard. Come on!'

Damian was now crying freely.

'I feel something awful has happened. Why isn't he here? I'm sorry, Dad.' Damian wiped his tears with the back of his glove and breathed deeply.

'I know how you feel, Dami. I'm not completely blind, you know.' Oliver put his arm round Dami's shoulder. 'I'm sure we'll find him.'

The wind was shifting to the south and the snow gave way to a light mist and drizzle as they made their descent through the cleft and came out on to the cove. The tide had been receding for some hours and a wide horseshoe of sand was visible beneath them. Oliver took the binoculars and climbed on to a ledge. Damian watched him slowly scanning the caves and rocky outcrops at the foot of the cliffs.

'There's something on the other side, on a clump of rock nearer the strand. It could be him,' Oliver said.

He jumped down to the sandy floor and they both raced across to the granite outcrop above the tideline.

Cos lay splayed on his back, his face grey and his eyes closed. Blood was caked round one knee. Damian knelt beside him, his tears spilling on to his face. Cos's eyes flickered as he bent down and kissed him.

'Cos, my darling, I thought... I was afraid...'

Oliver felt his pulse and wrapped him tightly in the insulating blanket. Cos's eyes opened and he looked at Damian and smiled.

'Thank God,' Oliver said. 'I'll check him over and then we must try to get him home. We could all die from exposure waiting for a helicopter today.'

***

Cos sat up and took the mug of chocolate from Damian, who sat on the edge of his bed. It was dark outside and the wind rattled the windows. Inside, the house was warm and delicious smells of cooking wafted up the stairs.

'I still feel so weird,' he said, 'like I've died and come back.'

'I'm so glad you did,' Damian said. 'Oliver wants to know if you're fit enough to come down for dinner. He said we should eat in the sitting room so you can lie on the sofa.'

'Yes, please, that would be heavenly.' Cos paused. 'Did you tell him?'

Damian held Cos's hand.

'You were right about Agincourt,' he said.

TIME TO BE A MAN
Edd Phillips

As the sun disappeared behind the hills and hedgerows, the single streetlight in the hamlet of Darting Brook flickered on, washing Clairsdown cottage with a shade of lollipop orange. Cracks lined the cottage's façade and paint peeled from the door-frame. In the bottom-floor windows, behind curtains thinned by age, black clad figures shifted to and fro.

Tom was standing in the back garden, hands in pockets. The grass, unkempt and tufty, soaked the bottoms of his black trousers with the remains of the day's earlier rain. He could hear the low mumble of voices from the living room and kitchen behind him. He had done his bit at the wake – shaking hands, listening to the stories and sympathies.

He took a deep draught of cold air and looked up at the first stars, expecting his grandad's face to smile back at him like one of those join-the-dot pictures of the zodiac signs. Nothing. Just stars.

He wandered off to the far end of the garden and reached the workshop that backed on to the lane behind. His grandad had told him that the building had housed pigs at one time. It still looked like it might. Tom approached the door – half hanging off its hinges, as it always had – lifted the stone frog on the step, removed the tarnished key from underneath and unlocked the padlock, which was more for show than anything.

The smell of WD40 and sawdust hit him as soon as he stepped inside. He flicked on the light switch and a strip light blinked in fits for ten seconds before settling. A bandsaw and pillar drill took up the centre of the room ahead of him, and, to his left and right, jutting from the walls, were two workbenches, their surfaces covered with pieces of wood, screws, boxes of nails, screwdrivers, a number of rulers, and pencils of various hardnesses. The remaining open stonework was either lined with shelving or had nails and hooks bored into it to support hacksaws, planes, sets of spanners and even an ancient wet-suit peppered with holes. Above, planks of ash, chestnut and yew, interspersed between sheets of plywood and metal, rested on the oak rafters, blocking the ceiling from view. Over twenty years Tom had been visiting that workshop. It had barely changed.

Past the bandsaw and pillar drill, on the opposite side of the room, was a set of double doors that could open out into the lane behind. In front of the doors was a rare piece of open space, usually reserved for what his grandad had called 'restoration and repair' projects: lawn-mowers, fridges, vacuum cleaners, an old lathe – whatever he could get his hands on for free or a favour. The last time Tom had seen his grandad he had been in that space, bent over a corroded water tank, his thin fingers, permanently stained by grease and tobacco, unscrewing a connector. Tom could see him clearly now – hair poking from his ears and nose, eyebrows connected in the middle, the bright whites of his wide eyes offset by coffee-brown irises. He had looked up at Tom and grinned with a smile like a broken zip. Who needed stars.

Tom strolled up to the pillar drill and pulled the handle, which still lowered the chuck smoothly. On his seventh birthday he had hidden under the work table of that same drill while playing hide-and-seek with his friends. Emelda had found him easily enough. Her auburn pigtails had bobbed up and down with glee and those freckles of hers that splashed the bridge of her nose and cheeks had been only inches from him. She'd tried to kiss him as punishment for choosing such a rubbish hiding place. But he had decided to run away instead and regretted that choice for most of his primary school days. When Emelda had moved towns later that same year, he'd cried for a whole day.

In the fringes of the light, at the far right-hand end of the workshop, Tom noticed a domed object hidden beneath a canvas tarpaulin. He couldn't take his eyes from it. His fingers twitched. As a boy, he had interrogated his grandad time and time again as to the mystery underneath that tarpaulin. When brave enough to creep his way over and steal a peek, Tom had always been caught and scolded, even when his grandad had seemed transfixed by his work ten seconds before.

Tom navigated his way between the pillar drill and right hand bench, after which he passed a rack with shelves bowed under the weight of pots of primer, emulsion, varnish, wax and wood stain. He paused before the metal table that supported the canvas-clad object and caressed the curve of the dome, mowing a path in the dust. His hand dropped to his side. He gripped a corner of the tarpaulin, began to edge it off, but let go. He took a step back and folded his arms. After a minute or so staring at it, he lunged forward and yanked off the tarpaulin with a flourish that cast a cloud of dust into the air and knocked over a margarine tub full of paintbrushes. Tom coughed, shielded his eyes and beat away the particles as they drifted down and settled on his clothes. The domed object before him shimmered in the light, its chromed surface distorting his reflection so that his nose seemed bulbous and his eyes appeared to bulge from their sockets. Whatever it was had been fashioned from a single sheet of metal, no joins visible, not a screw in sight. A sheet of A4 paper, covered in his grandad's jagged handwriting, flapped back and forth from where it was taped to the bottom of the device. Tom removed it, revealing a large, red button set into a panel above which the word ACTIVATE had been engraved in black.

Tom read the letter.

> Couldn't keep your grubby little paws off could you?
>
> I know there's only one person who would bother to come into my workshop and nose around after I've popped my clogs.
>
> Hello, Tom.

The corner of Tom's mouth curled up and was met by a tear.

> So you still want to know eh? Well, I have a feeling in my brittle old bones that my grand exit is drawing near, so I guess I ought to finally reveal all about this neat little contraption I've been working on for more years than I can remember.

This is my masterpiece.
This, my boy, is a time machine.

Tom looked from the letter to the gleaming object, then imagined the serious expression on his grandad's face. He couldn't help but chuckle.

Now, I know you may think this is me being a bit senile – which I am, true – but I assure you that this is the real deal. It's taken me many years to finish. I could've won a Nobel Prize by now if I had been brave enough to show anyone. Maybe there'll be a post-hummus one in it for me. Perhaps.

I have a feeling, though, that something like this might be too dangerous to show the world. So I thought I'd leave it up to you as to decide what to do with it. It's quite a basic contraption, to be honest. As instructions go, there's not much to it. Just that one button.

Tom wiped the tear from his cheek and glanced at the large, almost cartoonish, red button.

> I will warn you, though, I never tested this thing myself.
>
> I didn't want to be gallivanting about in time. I think I've hogged enough of that dimension already. I always imagined someone younger trying out this device and I would be more than happy if that person were you, Tom.
>
> So, if you wish to, go ahead and give it a try.
>
> But, as I said, this could be a dangerous thing. I never fully programmed it to be all that specific as to time and date and place and all that.
>
> The results, I imagine, will be a bit hit and miss.
>
> One push of that button and you could leap forward or back or crossways in time. You could change your life completely. Some people would give all they have for that.

But the question is, do you want to?
If you do, then go ahead.

This is my last gift to you.
Hope I wasn't too much of a pain in the posterior when I was alive.

All my love,
Grandad

Tom lowered the letter. He ran his hand over the metal – cool to the touch – and allowed his fingers to come to rest over the red button.

Once, his grandad had given him a piece of metal piping with a radio aerial attached. He had told Tom the object was a 'spirit-scope' and said that if he looked through it he would be able to see magical creatures like fairies and elves. Tom had been six, so obviously it had worked. When he became a teenager, the spirit-scope became a piece of metal piping once again.

Tom grinned. He had to give it to his grandad – the man had a sense of humour, even after death. He pushed the button.

What happened next Tom found hard to comprehend. He felt as if he had no physical body and was nothing but his mind floating in empty space. A sound much like the constant tolling of a bell rang in his non-existent ears. A burning smell filled his non-existent nostrils. White light blinded his non-existent eyes.

After what could have been a split second but equally years – impossible to tell – his body returned. Cool air on his skin. Feet on concrete floor. Daylight trickled through a window in the workshop wall, accompanied by giggles and shrieks of children in the garden outside. He turned around. The pillar drill and the bandsaw had grown. Quite significantly. The workbenches were higher – almost at head height – and the shelves appeared impossible for him to touch, let alone reach.

Tom held out his hands, backs facing him. His fingers had shrunk and all visible hair had disappeared from his arms and wrists. He stumbled forward a few steps and did not travel as far as he felt he should. When he looked down, he realized his legs were a third shorter than they used to be and that he was no longer wearing black trousers and his best brogues, but instead a pair of yellow shorts and blue and white trainers that had two Velcro straps to each. More worrying were his feet, which were less than half the size they used to be. No jacket and black tie either. He was wearing a red T-shirt with a stegosaurus on the front – a T-shirt he had been given as a present on his seventh birthday. A few years later, he had torn an irreparable hole in it when it had snagged on a nail on a fence in the Welsh hills.

But that hadn't even happened yet. Had it?

Seven-year-old Tom scrunched his brow. Who was he? Who was remembering these things? The man that he had been – the one with the mortgage, the fiancée, the car – was fast slipping away.

The door to the shed opened and a girl in a white dress entered.

'Found you!' she said.

Her auburn pigtails bobbed with glee as she ran towards him.

Emelda.

Tom backed away.

'You're rubbish at hiding,' she said.

Tom bumped against the metal table behind him.

'I think you should pay me for being such a rubbish hider.' Emelda crept forward on her toes, arms crossed behind her back. 'And I only like being paid with kisses.'

She bent forward, eyes closed, lips puckered. Those freckles – inches away.

Tom made to run, but hesitated. Some essence of that man he had been – braver than the boy – still lingered and clung on. Seven-year-old Tom made a half-smile and whispered under his breath, 'Thanks, Grandad.'

He leaned in and altered the course of time for evermore. No rumble of thunder sounded, no volcanoes exploded, no earthquakes. Simply the squeak of little lips marked the occasion.

That last essence of manhood relinquished its grip on Tom and dissipated like smoke on the wind, leaving just a boy kissing Emelda from down the road.

He never knew of the resultant ripples in time that he had caused – how that one choice altered the very fabric of the universe from then on. There again, nobody else noticed either. Every being in the universe continued living, quite obliviously, on a brand-new path.

Tom spent many days of his boyhood with his grandad, who tinkered away with all manner of machinery in his workshop. The boy left no nook or cranny of that space unexplored, apart from one spot, where a domed object, cloaked by a canvas tarpaulin, evaded his most stealthy attempts to unveil it. One day he'd find out what lay beneath. Even if it took twenty years.

VANAMO
Fleur Jeremiah

The cabin, made of grey logs of deadwood, blended into the landscape as if it had roots in the soil, like the pine trees and spruces at the foot of the fell. Linnea inhaled the fresh air. It was not far from midsummer and, though it was approaching eleven o'clock, the road through the wood was sunlit. The Lapp air felt cool compared to Helsinki. A lone reindeer was chewing at a sapling; he must have temporarily strayed from his herd. He paused to look at her before the antlers went down again as he continued nibbling, obviously used to tourists.

 A cluster of pink by the side of the road caught Linnea's eye. She let go of her small case and crouched down to take a better look at the tiny bell-like flowers she had been named after, to catch their fragrance, which was surprisingly strong at night and reminiscent of lilac. The powerful scent wafted from the delicate blossoms, disproportionate like the song produced by a nightingale from its slight frame.

Vanamo, the Finnish name of the plant, had been her mother's favourite flower. 'Just as it was the favourite of Carl von Linné, the Swedish botanist who gave it its Latin name, *Linnaea borealis*,' she'd told the small Linnea. 'Think of the great man having such a delicate favourite among all the plants of the world.' She had decided to call her twin daughters Linnea and Vanamo. They would be a twinflower – she had discovered the English name from some tourists at the spa hotel in Luosto – and stay together like the 'paired blooms, pendulous pale pink corollas at the end of a short stem'. She had shown them a picture and read the words from her *Guide to Finnish Wild Flowers*.

Linnea dug her fingers deeper into the moss to trace the slender, vertical, hidden part of the stem that extended beyond the reach of her hand and forearm. She remained still, until aching knees forced her to stand up and continue her walk to the cabin.

She loved the smell of timber that welcomed her into the spacious living room furnished with simple wooden furniture, all pine: a dining table, four chairs, an upholstered armchair and a settee. A wood-burning stove in the corner was filled with logs ready to be lit. After unpacking, she warmed a piece of pizza in the microwave installed above the electric cooker and sat down at the table by the window with a bottle of Lapin Kulta, her favourite beer. It was now past eleven, but the sky was still blue and the trees cast their shadows as if it were a summer's day. She watched a solitary lemming scuttle past the side of the cabin and listened to the silence.

Pity she had to find him. There had to be better ways for a twenty-year-old to spend her holidays.

In the morning, as she drank her coffee, she felt a presence beside her. When she turned her head, the phantom was not there. She felt she had company all the way as she walked along the forest path to the nearby hotel, the Amethyst Spa. She tried to push the ghostly presence away, turning suddenly to see if she could catch it, but it was too elusive. When she got to the end of the short cut and stood in front of the low sprawling hotel, also made of logs, the presence evaporated. Lucky the path had been deserted, or she might have been arrested for being drunk and disorderly at worst; at best she would have attracted some unwanted attention.

A herd of reindeer was standing around in the car park, close to a few German tourist buses that would be on their way further north, probably to Inari. A couple of smokers were having an animated conversation in Swedish on the wide wooden steps leading to the reception. Linnea squared her shoulders as she walked past them to the reception desk, which was located at the end of a passage with a display of merchandise: Sami hats, I ♥ Lapland T-shirts and sweaters, toy huskies and wolves, patterned jumpers. You could see the swirling waters of the spa area through a glass wall; a couple of computer screens near the wall offered a virtual tour of the Luosto amethyst mines, where you could go and find your very own piece of amethyst, carefully planted, like in an Easter egg hunt.

Linnea stood still for a while, looking round the foyer, watching the receptionist, a mature woman with chubby arms, glasses and dark, straight hair. Her white blouse was too small for her and the buttons threatened to burst open as she turned to pick up some papers from the desk behind her.

'Linnea!' The woman stood up.
'Marja... Is he still here?'
'Is it Jaakko you're talking about?'
'Who else?'
'Is that wise?'
'Wise is not the point. Where is he? Does he still work for you?'

'No. Drank too much. Got too old to scrub the floors and change the barrels.'

'Where is he? I know you know where. I'll find him. Just make it easy for me.'

'Linnea... How's Helsinki? Do you miss the fell?'

'Where is he?'

A voice behind Linnea: *'Entschuldigen Sie, aber...'* One of the German buses was about to leave, a queue was building up behind her.

'He lives in a derelict yellow wooden house by the Kitisenjoki. It's not far from the bridge, on the bank opposite the school... behind the Piitsi bar.'

'Thanks. See you.'

Linnea stepped aside to make way for the foot-tapping German tour guide.

The river stood still, or so it seemed, like a wide, winding mirror reflecting the sky, the clouds, the sun, the dark trees where they grew close to the water's edge further upstream. Linnea leaned against the railings of the bridge and stared at the reflection. When she looked hard enough, she could see a slight shifting and distortion of the pattern on the water's surface: the calm and wide Kitisenjoki was never quite still, without a current or a ripple as it stretched out toward the horizon and melted into the sky. If there was anything she missed it was this; if only she could transport herself here every so often, stay for half an hour and then go back to the excitement and bustle of her busy job in Helsinki. She lifted her right arm as if to place it on the shoulder of someone next to her.

'Vanamo, I miss you.'

A passing cyclist gave her a searching look and she shook herself as if coming to. The yellow house was visible on the far river bank, she headed towards it.

* * *

Nobody seemed to know who actually owned the derelict cottage. It was in a prime location by the river, close to the man-made beach. The paint was peeling and one of the windows had a hole covered with a piece of cardboard. A tree was working its way up towards the sky from the chimney. The outhouse, the same yellow, was in a worse state, leaning to one side, its total collapse imminent. The space between the two buildings was covered in long grass and showy yellow globe flowers. A gravel path led to the house.

Linnea stood by the front door and knocked. No reply. She knocked again; this time, a growling noise came from inside. An invitation to enter? Maybe. She turned the handle and pushed the door, which opened with a loud creak. She found herself in a tiny hallway beside a filthy rag rug and a pair of wellingtons, looking into a room which seemed dark after the bright daylight – the windows were small and dirty, one of them partially covered by cardboard. It took a few moments for Linnea's eyes to adjust: a half-dead geranium on one of the windowsills, a wooden table, a bench and a chair, and in the chair an old man. In front of him, a bottle of spirits and a half-empty glass. A bed with a surprisingly bright patchwork quilt was next to the wall behind him.

The man made an attempt to stand but dropped back on to his seat. He then tried to sit up straight with some success, and put his fingers through his straggly hair. His face was round, his complexion ruddy, with bags under his eyes. The eyes were surprisingly blue, not faded at all, and there was a hint of the old charm somewhere there in the stocky body.

'And is it really my Linnea, come to see her old dad? Come in, come in. Take a seat.'

Linnea stepped in and sat down opposite the man. A tear was trickling down his face. She turned away to stare at the geranium.

'That plant needs watering.'

'Is that all you've got to say to your old dad. Five years and not a word...'

They sat without speaking until a scratching noise broke the silence. A tabby cat emerged from under the bed and began sharpening her claws on the floorboards.

'Come on, old girl. Misu's all I've got...' The cat twirled round his legs and dashed to the door. 'She's a good mouser, gets her own food and keeps the place free of pests.'

He was quite animated. His hand moved towards the glass and the bottle.

'Fancy a drink? I've got another glass somewhere... I don't get many visitors.' He attempted a laugh.

'No, thanks. You carry on.'

She stood abruptly, filled a cracked mug with water from a sink in the corner and walked to the wilting geranium. 'It's probably too late. It's probably dead.' She poured the water on top of the soil in the pot, but most of it flowed over the edge or was left swirling on the hard surface. 'Definitely too late. Why don't you throw the bloody thing out?'

'I will, I will.'

The man's body slumped forward, his forehead nearly touching the table.

She came back and sat down again. She patted the space next to her and stretched out her arm to one side as if to place it on someone's shoulders.

'You killed Vanamo,' she said. 'My sister.'

'What? What the hell –'

'You killed her... You never loved her. You killed her, you –'

The old man leapt up and thumped the table. 'Shut your bloody mouth! You have no fucking idea... I DID NOT kill her. She slipped away. She wanted to swim on her own. She wanted to be strong, wanted to swim just like you did.'

He fell back into his chair and covered his face. He grabbed the bottle for another swig.

Linnea stood up. 'Come on, Vanamo. We'd better go.'

She headed for the door, holding the hand of her sister. They went outside into the sunshine, where the river was glimmering, the beach deserted. Too cold for a swim today. Linnea sat on the wooden jetty and looked at the river.

'Bye, Vanamo.' And, after a moment, 'Bye, Dad. I wish...'

Linnea recalled Vanamo's special chair. It had pink and white stripes, and Linnea had wanted one too. But then Mum had made her realize it was better to be able to walk than have a special chair, however pretty. Dad and Linnea were the athletic ones in the family.

Dad acted as a guide on walks to the amethyst mine, climbing the path 'like a mountain goat' – that's what Linnea thought. She had had a picture book which told the story of a goat with massive horns, able to climb any mountain and rescue people in distress. Sometimes she saw him watching Vanamo with an odd look. Mum's eyes were always warm when she looked at her twin sister, but Dad... it was not hatred, not pity, not love... Linnea couldn't quite put her finger on it. Vanamo was clever and good with her hands and she won a drawing competition with a picture of a reindeer and the northern lights, but Dad didn't say anything. Mum pinned the picture on the kitchen wall and said it kept her company and made her happy when she was cooking.

Dad thought that Vanamo could walk if she tried hard enough. Once he picked her up and held her upright and told her to put some weight on her leg to make it stronger. Vanamo began to cry and Mum rushed to the scene, white-faced, and Dad sat the tearful child back in her special chair with that funny look of his, while Mum promised the girls they could help her with the baking tonight. They both loved it and Linnea cut a star with a pastry cutter for her twin and Vanamo shaped a little girl from the dough with just her hands, for her hands were nimble.

They were eight when Vanamo drowned. She wasn't a strong swimmer: though she could stay afloat and paddle a bit, she couldn't kick very well. Mum worked part-time and had a couple of evening shifts. It was a warm summer evening and Dad said he would take the girls for a swim; they would go to the beach by the Kitisenjoki and have a splash in the shallow bit. The beach was deserted, as most people were having their dinner. Linnea ran into the water and Dad lifted Vanamo out of her chair and helped her change and gently carried her to the water's edge. Linnea could see her large blue, trusting eyes, and then she turned away to swim. She was a strong swimmer and knew what was safe. And then... her mind went blank; later, an image of her sister's lifeless body, her mother crying, her Dad's silent, stony face. Her sister was gone. And her Dad.

Helsinki seemed full of bustle as Linnea walked along the coast road to Cafe Ursula. Cyclists were out in force, whizzing past her, the evening sun behind their backs. Her friends were already there, seated at their favourite table with a splendid view of the sea.

Sirkka, Leena and Linnea met here a couple of times every summer. Sirkka had dyed her hair black and was wearing leggings and a bright top, a bit like a smock; Leena wore one of her long bright dresses with a design of red poppies and a matching scarf to hold back her hair.

'Linnea! Did you meet many handsome reindeer herders?'

Sirkka couldn't quite buy into the idea of a retreat, of burying yourself in a forest. On the other hand, Leena, a counsellor, was keen on the spiritual dimension of her friend's journey, as she called it. And Linnea told them about the beauty of the forest and the river and threw in a handsome German tourist for Sirkka's benefit, as the three friends sat there in the sun by the sea.

THE SHADOW
Ruth Cohen

I know now of course that the waiting will end soon. It feels as if time has contracted and my whole life has been a preparation for this moment. I am no longer fit for work and indeed have no desire to return to it. I am consumed with the present and provided I do not think too hard I am dully content, passing time, pacing the room and staring out of the window. Yesterday elides into tomorrow and what has been is no longer relevant. Even my beloved writers speak of matters which no longer concern me and I find little solace in their company. I am, at last, completely alone.

It began about six months ago in late February when teaching English in a further education college. I was not altogether comfortable in the post. I did not wish to integrate into the life of the college and found it difficult to motivate the students towards the classical texts that I loved. However, it suited me geographically and I found the work easy, if somewhat frustrating. The multi-sited college was located in south London and that evening I was staying late doing some marking in one of those Victorian school buildings with high ceilings and separate entrances for boys and girls. The second-floor room I occupied was furnished with individual tables and a whiteboard and overlooked a bare concrete playground. I missed the old desks with holes for inkwells that resonated of happier days, and the evocative smell of chalk and gym shoes that had been replaced by one of furniture polish. However, my wife had died the previous year and, in no hurry to go home now, I relished my own company. Some colleagues were meeting later in a local pub but I had no inclination to join them. They had little affection for me, nor I for them, and I found their preoccupation with what they called modern culture tedious in the extreme. I worked well into the evening before I realized that it was getting dark. I had not been aware of the hour but now the dusky light reminded me of time passing.

A shadow loomed across the window and hovered for a moment, as if peering in. Odd, I thought, and rose to investigate – but it quickly vanished. There were no trees or traffic outside and I could see nothing that might have caused it. However, some imperative drove me to close the exercise books and make my way out. It was late and, using my master key, I exited the building by the glow of the lamps in the car park. As I walked towards my car, I saw Joe, the caretaker, hurrying towards me. He was almost running – no mean feat for a man of his bulk. I waited for him to catch up with me. As he drew closer he was screwing up his eyes as if he couldn't see clearly, although the lighting was bright enough.

'Mr Atkins? Is that you?'

'Peter,' I said automatically.

I was forever trying to get him to address me by my first name. I disapproved of the social distinction reflected in the use of titles, though I sometimes wished that my students did not hold the same principles.

'Mr Peter, I thought you'd gone. I've locked the gates.'
'No. Sorry to have held you up.'
'But I saw you.'
'Saw me?'
'Yes, saw you leave half an hour ago.'

He was panting now, red-faced, his bald head gleaming in the lamplight.

'Can't have been me.'
'But it was you. I'd know that jacket anywhere, and your, er, walk.' He meant my limp.
'You must have been mistaken.'

He shook his head.

'No. I'm sure it was you, and you waved at me.'

The man was stubborn and wouldn't let go. We stared at each other in the gloom. Then he muttered something and turned away, rattling his keys pointedly as he moved to reopen the car park.

I got in my car, a rather battered Peugeot, and drove home, trying to put the incident out of my mind. Yet I felt unaccountably rattled, and when I got home I opened a bottle of Chilean Merlot and poured a large glass, drinking most of it standing in the kitchen before refilling it and settling in a chair with a sigh of relief. I remember picking up a photo of Sarah which I'd knocked on the floor and staring at it, as if she could provide some explanation.

Looking back, of course, I see now that was not really the beginning, just the beginning of the end. There were a number of trivial things subsequently, which singly meant little, but put together became increasingly disturbing. Most of them revolved around mistaken identity, people like Joe seeing me in places which I had not visited. Then about ten days after the incident with Joe, the Head of Department met me in the corridor. She was a brisk, no-nonsense woman whom I rather admired.

'Oh, Peter, how are you?' she said.

'Well, thank you.' I was not going to say 'good'.

'What a surprise seeing you,' she continued. 'You've recovered very quickly.'

'Recovered?'

'You sounded dreadful on the phone.' She stopped and put a hand on my arm. 'You really must take care of yourself. I've got your classes covered as you asked, so go home.' She put on a mock stern face, pretending to frown, and patted me again. 'Must fly.' She swept off, her blue cape flowing behind her like a standard.

I was alarmed. I remembered no phone call. Although unaware of having upset anyone more than usual, I assumed that someone must be playing a cruel joke, imitating me. I was suspicious and eyed my colleagues with increasing wariness. People began to look at me oddly and one day someone deliberately moved my chair in the English Department's section of the staffroom to one side, isolating it from the others. When I commented on this to a senior staff member who also taught literature, a man to whom I had been closer than anyone else in the college, he told me I was overreacting. I felt more and more like an outsider.

Two or three weeks passed like this and it was nearly the end of term. The catalyst happened on the last day of March. It was 4.30 and I had been trying to instil an appreciation of Milton into an unwilling group of A-level students. I wanted them to admire Milton's description of Satan, and how he depicted the beauty of sin. They were shuffling and uninterested and when I eventually dismissed them I felt as dispirited as I had ever been. I succumbed to a moment of weakness and laid my head down on the desk in front of me. I had been thinking a lot lately about Sarah. I would not admit to guilt but wondered if my behaviour had been questionable, my treatment of her even brutal.

'Oh, Sarah,' I said out loud.

I heard the door creak open and the heavy footsteps of a

man cross the bare floor and stop in front of me.
'Yes?' I mumbled, ashamed to raise my head.
No answer.
'Yes?'
Still no answer.
'For God's sake.'
I lifted my head in time to see a figure leaving the room. There was something horribly familiar about its presence. Surely I knew those jeans, that aftershave and that walk, Christ, yes, that walk... I began shivering uncontrollably.

That night I went straight home. I closed the blinds, drew all the curtains and turned on all the lights. The house was an old Edwardian property in what estate agents would call a mixed neighbourhood. Now that Sarah had gone, the place felt much too big for me and a move seemed the obvious option. But something had held me there, preventing me from looking seriously at alternatives. I was still shaking and when I looked in the mirror my reflection seemed distorted, wild-eyed, my greying hair standing up in tufts. Was I having a breakdown? Was I psychotic? I did not know what to do, where to turn. The house seemed impossibly large and eerie, and oddly shaped shadows hung around the dusty corners, despite all the blazing lights. I picked up the phone, replaced the receiver, picked it up again. I am a rational man, however, and decided that I must be having a panic attack. Who could I call? There was no one left now who really knew me and the police would laugh at me. I considered ringing the Samaritans and perhaps that's what I should have done. But I opted for alcohol and eventually fell into a whisky coma, punctuated by strange dreams in which I was continually running from something behind me, only to anticipate it lurking ahead around the next corner.

I awoke at dawn, curled up on the floor of the sitting room, stale and dishevelled and half buried in cushions from the sofa. My body was chilled and trembling slightly, but I felt more in control of myself. The rooms were still brightly lit, the curtains and blinds drawn from the night before, and I opened everything up to let in the pale morning light. I drank a glass of orange juice from the fridge and opened the back door to the garden. Everything was still that morning and I could hear birds chanting their early matins. I stepped out and on to the grass, wet with morning dew. Now it was Eliot's cruellest month and the ground was quickening with life, small shoots rising from the earth, early buds beginning to adorn the bare branches. I walked over to the vegetable patch which Sarah had so carefully cultivated. I remembered her then with something approaching sorrow. I gazed at the earth, rich brown and peaty, and mourned her. Oh, Sarah, what have I done?

A sudden breeze stirred the foliage and the air grew colder. I wrapped my arms around myself to keep warm as clouds scudded across the sky. The garden grew silent as the birds stopped singing. A scent of mould filled my nostrils. Winter is making a comeback: I spoke the words out loud and started again to shiver. Something scuttled in the dead leaves and it was then I knew the awful truth that it was standing there behind me.

After what seemed an eternity I gave way to the inevitable and turned to face my pursuer. Without surprise I saw myself: grey hair unkempt, worn blue sweater, cuffs slightly frayed. Strangely, then, my fear dissipated, leaving behind what was almost a sense of relief. We looked at each other, my doppelgänger and I, and as I started to make my way back to the house I saw that he did also. We strolled together up the garden path and together entered the building. But once inside, when I turned towards him again, he was gone.

I have not seen him since, but I know that he will return. Waiting for death is a curious business. If you had asked me last year what it would feel like to know you yourself were about to die, I would probably have shrugged and given some sort of flippant reply. After all, at sixty-four I am still young enough not to see the skull beneath the skin at every turn, though now that day is not so far away. The strange thing is, the closer it comes, the less fearful I feel. A sort of fatalism has overtaken me and most of the time I am calm. Only occasionally, in the black watches of the night, I hear a rustling in the darkness and then a dreadful terror overwhelms me.

FLIRTING WITH DANGER
Annette Caseley

When Jim asks about him, the one I have managed to eradicate most traces of, I know that trouble is not far away. I should confess, but I can't face it. I don't want my efforts in covering everything up to have been in vain.

'Alex was special,' I admit.

Dark brown eyes, long lashes, pale skin with cute freckles and a cheeky smile which made him look less innocent than he was at twenty. We met at drama school, but he dropped out in the second year to find a new life.

I stop for a moment and glance across the bar at Jim. Jim McCarthy, if that's even his real name. He's attractive – mid-thirties, thick jet-black hair – and I can tell he works out by the well-defined arm muscles, lean rather than bulky. Under his tight white T-shirt his stomach is flat, so I guess he's careful about his weight, which explains why he's not drinking as much as I am.

We were introduced at Fred's party last week. He flirted with me and we discussed the terrible state that the UK film industry is in. My interest was piqued when he mentioned he was a director, but even more so when he revealed that he had funding for a new film. Now funding, that's the hardest part for a director.

'Full funding,' he said. He teased me with, 'there might be a part in it for you.'

Because he paid for all the drinks, I believed him and ignored the voice in my head that told me to be careful. I pretended not to be alarmed when he explained that the film was about a couple searching for their lost son. I told myself it was a coincidence.

I should never have agreed to meet him again tonight, but I need to be in this film. I should leave, but Jim's come-to-bed eyes are not easy to avoid and it's been a long time since my last relationship.

'What's my part?' I enquire.

'I think you'd be good as the son's girlfriend,' he says.

When I ask why, he gives me some bullshit about knowing that I would be able to convey how desperate the girlfriend feels after the disappearance, and understand the parents' daily torture of not knowing what happened. Jim makes me want to tell him about Alex. I have wanted to tell someone for years and Alex's parents should know.

Alex and I moved into this large one-bedroom flat in Kentish Town, posh road opposite a park, high ceilings, huge sash windows, wooden floors, all financed by his mum and dad: uptight Mary and religious Andrew. Alex wanted to be an actor and he had struck a deal with his wealthy parents. They would pay for his acting course, but if within two years of completing it he had no work as an actor, he would join a 'proper' profession.

'I've heard about Alex. Were you close?' Jim asks.

I want to tell him that two people have never been closer.

Alex and I were inseparable. Wherever he went, I went. I was nothing before he came along. He bought me dresses from Selfridges, advised me on my hair, convinced me to bare my legs and wear high-heeled shoes.

'Sandra, you're a beautiful woman,' he'd say as he observed me in the mirror which hung in our hallway. No one has ever loved me like that. With his guidance and his parents' money, I became Sandra, the Beauty Queen.

Jim kisses my hand. 'Sandra, Sandra, what a beautiful name.'

I laugh at his corny line, but I don't tell him it's short for Alexandra. I dare my hand to touch his arm and I smile when he doesn't remove it. How much does he suspect me?

'So, what are you going to call this film, then?' I ask.

'*How to End the Pain.*'

'Because?'

'Because the parents hire a private investigator to find out about their son's fate.'

'I don't like the title.'

'What would you suggest?'

'*Flirting with Danger* sounds more enticing, don't you think?'

He doesn't answer, but kisses my hand and his lips move their way up my arm and shoulder. I pretend to be embarrassed by the stares of other drinkers and stop him before he tries to remove the red silk scarf I have round my neck.

Alex's parents would never have accepted me. They didn't approve of arty types. I knew Alex wouldn't stay, that he'd always planned to leave.

'We should go to your place,' Jim whispers.

I don't want to: he might find traces of my past with Alex.

In the black cab on our way to his hotel, I unbutton my shirt and tease him with a flash of the breasts that I am not shy to flaunt. He's interested, I can tell, but how interested?

In his room, I unzip his trousers and I'm pleased with his size.

'Now that we're so intimate, tell me: what did you do with all the money?' Jim asks.

I want to laugh, because he's feeling my surgically enhanced bosom. Does he not realize he's close to what he's looking for?

'Alex needed the cash to leave. He'd been making regular withdrawals.'

'I know,' Jim says as I hold his cock with my left hand. 'Maybe you helped him?'

I should be scared: he's done his research.

He kisses me gently on the lips and moves his hands over my breasts. The silky fabric of my skirt against his skin is having a positive effect.

I used to withdraw money from the cashpoint when Alex and I were still an item. Mary and Andrew have enough to last three generations so I don't feel guilty. I feel entitled to it. Maybe I was careless one night and Jim saw me on some CCTV camera. I knew the pin number and helped myself. Alex approved. I even signed a few cheques before he left. Alex wanted me to have those operations and keep the flat.

'Do you like my breasts?' I ask. 'I used the best surgeon money could buy.'

Jim mumbles appropriately and kisses each nipple, the left one and then the right. He moves his head away to admire my large breasts, a hand under each, and says, 'Good work,' as if he was Dr Melville from Harley Street himself.

I don't inform him that Dr Melville had to operate many more times before he reached perfection.

'So tell me more about the film,' I whisper as I remove my blouse completely. 'Do the parents find their son?'

He removes his shirt and now I can feel his skin brush against my breasts.

'The scriptwriter wasn't sure how to end the story,' Jim says.

'Alex was a troubled young man, you know,' I tell him.

Jim nods. As I look down, I notice the white line instead of a tan where his wedding ring would be. I don't care. I want him. I've not been this excited by the prospect of a man for a long time.

'Were you surprised when Alex left?' Jim asks.

I'm honest and say, 'No. He'd been planning to disappear for a long time.'

Once I'd realized my true potential and beauty, Alex paid for me to get into the most exclusive London clubs, and he loved the effect I had on other men there. At five foot eleven with heels, I made an immediate impression. I became more powerful, more demanding. That's why Alex is no longer here: I left no space for him.

'Where are your parents from, Sandra?'

'My parents are dead,' I say, teasing because I know he's not been able to trace them.

We have reached the bed now. I'm grateful we didn't end up in the flat, the same bed I shared with Alex. I wonder: would that have scared Jim?

'Where did you get your surname, Lear, from?'

'It's a stage name. Every actress has one.'

I watch Jim's eyes – cobalt blue like the sea. He's starting to slur his words, the effect of something I added to his drink. I should stop this now. Jim's getting too close, he's dangerous – the voice inside is warning me to walk out. You got away with it. Don't ruin it now.

It would all have been different if his family had accepted me. They could have saved themselves years of pain. Deep down, they must know they are to blame. Should I tell Jim about Alex? How far is Jim willing to take this? Is he being paid enough to have sex with the likes of me?

I make sure my handbag is close to the bed – I might need it soon. Jim takes a condom out of his wallet.

I laugh. 'I can't get pregnant. No need to use that thing.'

Jim hesitates. I take the condom from him, still in its wrapper, toss it across the bed and it lands on the floor.

Jim walks round the bed and bends down to retrieve it from the carpet. 'Better safe than sorry.'

There's no point arguing. Jim lies on the bed, leans across to reach my hands and pulls me towards him.

'Is that why Alex left you?'

That shocks me. Perhaps I should tell the bastard what I did with Alex and how I got rid of his body. I want to hurt Mary and Andrew, who never accepted me. I shouldn't let Jim rattle me like this. I'm scared to say anything in case my voice betrays me. Instead, I shrug my shoulders and join him on the bed.

Soon he's naked, but I'm still clothed from the waist down: skirt, suspenders and knickers.

'So,' he whispers again, 'what did you do with all that money? Did you bury it with his body?'

Is that why he is here? For the money rather than finding Alex? I can help him with both. I slide my knickers off.

'La Perla,' I say, dangling them in front of his face before I toss them aside and climb on top of him.

His lips are inviting and I reach down to taste them. I stretch to grab my handbag and pull it on to the bed. Jim tenses.

'Just something to help us,' I say.

I open the bag and show him the baby oil. I don't want my inability to lubricate to ruin this night of passion.

'What did you do with the money?' he asks after I have greased his cock.

We're both hiding behind our disguises. I am aroused by this charade and I haven't had such fun in years. I sense he's getting close and soon he's in. The musical twang of the bedsprings and our breathing fills the room.

'Jimmy.' I think I am allowed to call him that now. 'Jimmy. Oh, Jimmy –' as I ride up and down – 'you've just found what I did with the money.'

BIG LOVE
Colin Harlow

I was busy clearing up after breakfast. My G (Geoff) had just eaten six chickens, two pigs and half a cow. Feathers, bones and trotters lay discarded across a knotted oak table. I swept the detritus with a yard brush into refuse sacks. Big blokes can be such messy eaters, especially when they are in a rush to get to work. As he kissed me goodbye, chicken blood, pig and cow juices dribbled through his beard on to my neck and rested in the crevice of my cleavage.

After G had left there was a knock at the door. I opened it. Outside stood a young boy with shoulder-length dark curly hair and eyes as blue as the winding road that led from the clouds beyond the hills. His skin was pale, translucent. He had raw scratches on his bare shins. He wore knee-length, rust-coloured corduroy trousers with an oversized white shirt belted round his middle with a frayed chequered tie. Odd laces pulled up worn walking boots.

'Good morning, Mrs,' he said, a toothy smile beaming across his face. His lips were crimson red and full. 'I'm almost dizzy from hunger. Please, could you find it in your soul to give me something to eat?'

My heart pounded. How could I refuse a creature with such fine alabaster features who was so polite and oh so minute?

'You'd best get yourself in here,' I said, ushering him into the house. 'There be wild roaming giants round these parts who would eat anything.' I wrapped a finger round one of his ebony curls. 'Even well-mannered boys.'

I closed the door behind us, then picked him up and placed him on the knotted oak table while I began to cook. He looked as if he hadn't eaten in weeks.

'What you doing in Bigdom?' I asked. 'Normally we only ever sees giants from the other winding roads.'

'I've come from Smalldom, travelling for hours up a marigold that reaches from there to here,' he said.

'This be no place for a child,' I said. 'A lot of giants round these parts is partial to small boys, no matter be they good or bad, but especially the wicked ones who are that little bit more dangerous.'

His eyes were wide while I cooked, as if he was trying his best to stay awake.

'What is your name, boy?'

'Will,' he said.

'Be you a good or a wicked boy, Will?'

He winked at me.

'In that case you is very welcome here, to eat as much as you wants and stay for as long as you wishes.'

I placed a bowl of seasoned potage in front of him and chunks of baked bread. He slurped the soup like a dog lapping up water and tucked into the bread as if he be a bird eating every berry from a tree.

The table and house began to shake; G was on his way.

Will's blue eyes began to fill with tears.

'Don't be scared. Nothing bad will happen to you while you is with me,' I said as I picked him up off the table and wiped his eyes, and I tasted his tears as I put my finger to my mouth and motioned for him to be quiet.

The footsteps were getting nearer and louder. The door handle turned. I placed Will in the oven and left it open a fraction. He would be able to see how lovely my G was.

G opened the door and came into the house. He sat at the table, looked around, smiled and said, 'I smell the blood of an innocent, one still young, vulnerable and true.'

'You is right, my handsomest. We do have ourselves a beautiful visitor.'

I opened the oven door and held Will in my arms. He was still trembling and crying silently. I placed him on the table in front of G.

'Will's his name,' I said.

G twisted a finger round one of Will's ebony curls and stroked his cheek. 'Hello,' he said. 'You is indeed most lovely. I do think it be time for us all to celebrate.'

Will smiled as we took him from the table, held him in our arms and danced round the kitchen for hours. He laughed with merriment and shouted, 'More, more.' A smile never left his face. His eyes stayed wide open.

When we finished, we sat on upholstered floating cushions, Will nestled between us. We asked him what time he had to be home, as it was getting late and dark. Will said it didn't matter because his mother wouldn't be in anyway. She'd be off out with her men friends, working to feed his ungrateful mouth.

'Since Father died we haven't had much money and Mother does what she has to. That's why I'm in Bigdom,' he said, 'to see if I can find any extra money to help her out.'

G and I listened to Will's tale, looked at each other and nodded. G got down from the cushions, went to our bedroom and returned a few minutes later with a small bag of silver florins. We told Will to take the money so it would help his mother put food on the table. He began to cry again.

'Nobody's ever been this kind to me. How will I ever be able to thank you?'

We put our arms around him. 'There's no need to thank us. Just come and visit whenever you want,' I said. 'You is always most welcome.' We looked at the clock and saw it was getting late. 'We'll take you to the end of the winding road so you can go down your marigold safely.'

That night G and I lay in bed wrapped round each other, his breath resting around my neck, his hands searching my desires. I thought about Will and hoped he'd arrived home safely and prayed we would see him again soon.

A couple of weeks later G and me had just finished having a bath when there was a knock at the door. G went to see who it was.

'Matilda, we got ourselves a visitor,' he said.

Will ran towards me. I picked him up and twirled him around, while he held on to my ears, kissing me.

'I've missed you,' he said.

Ah, children can be such charming liars.

'I've got something to show you both.'

We sat on the cushions to see what he had brought. Will's chest did come right open, as a minute purple velvet-covered song-book fell from his heart and on to his lap. While he turned the pages letters began to edge off the side, looped into figures of eight and turned into lily-winged butterflies. Soon the room was full with a darting spectacle.

'I remembered you like to dance,' Will said.

G and I leaned over and squeezed his knees. 'We do indeed love to dance.'

All three of us spent the rest of the afternoon flying with the letters.

* * *

We rested a while.

'Matilda,' Will said, 'is there any more games we could all play together?'

'There be something,' I said. ''Tis a special game that can be played any time you comes to visit. 'Tis also a secret game just between us three.'

'Secret games are the best,' Will said, giving one of his toothy grins.

We sat next to each other, Will resting between us on both our knees. We held him tight.

'Close your eyes, Will,' I said, 'and hold out your hands.'

When the game had finished, G went outside to the garden, while Will and I lay on the floor, his body held in mine as I tousled those fine locks. G returned with Clara, our prized golden-egg-laying hen.

'This is a special gift for you, Will,' G said, 'especially for you and your mother. Any time you needs anything just tell Clara here to lay you a golden egg. Your poor mother will never have to work again.'

Will began to hug us. 'Oh, Mother will be eternally happy.'

'We will also be eternally happy if you comes back often and plays our game again,' I said.

Will smiled. 'I will,' he said, as his eyes began to close another time before he left for Smalldom.

G and I slept like untoucheds that night, content with the memory of Will and our afternoon together.

Dear Will kept his promise and returned a couple of days later. He soon started to visit us every day after school. We never did ask or beg – he come of his own free will. Each afternoon it was him who'd always ask to play our game. Most of the time we'd all play together, but sometimes it would be just Will and me while G sat and watched. I would always smile at G while I pleasured Will with the gaps between my teeth. Before Will left us every night we'd always give him a little something to take back to Smalldom. Some trinket for him and his mother. We wanted to thank her for letting Will come as often as he did.

One Saturday afternoon Will arrived with flowering edible tulips he had grown specially for us. They did remind us of the tenderness of his fresh skin. That afternoon was the most memorable and special we did ever had, and as a treat we decided to show Will our musical harp. G brought it into the living room, placed it on the floor and let the crystal strings begin to play. As usual the sounds were intoxicating and we were each transported into our own dreams of delicacies and desires. When we woke up, Will had an enormous smile.
'Did you enjoy that?' I asked.
'It's the best place I've ever been,' Will replied.
'That harp is the most valuable and precious possession any giant could have and there be only three left in the kingdom,' I said. 'We have to keep that a secret too. Otherwise, folk would be wanting to enter into their dreams and unfulfilled desires.'
Will looked at us. 'Can I lie between you?'
We could never refuse him anything. While Will lay between us, his hands discovering us both, he said, 'You do love me, don't you?'
'Of course we do, little one,' I said.
'Do you love me enough to give me anything I want?' he asked.
'If we have it, Will, then 'tis as good enough yours,' G said.
'In that case, I'd like to have the crystal harp,' he said as his hands squeezed into ours.
G and I glanced at each other, tears rolling down our cheeks.
'Dear, dear beautiful boy,' I said. 'We do love you like we never have the others, but this we cannot do. That harp must always stay with us.'
Will began to sob uncontrollably. 'You said you loved me.'
We held him tight, close to our breathing pulses, hoping his

tender breath would always rest on ours. We knew it couldn't.

Will wiped his eyes. 'Can I at least stay the night and return to Smalldom tomorrow?'

We were of course delighted. That evening we played our treasured game once more and as a final goodnight treat listened to the harp while we all fell asleep.

Halfway through the night we could hear a cry. G and I both woke up sweating. Will wasn't to be seen in our bed.

'Master, master, help me,' the harp screamed.

We raced out of the bedroom. Will was leaving through the front door with the harp around his shoulder.

'Will, don't you dare leave here, you filthy child.'

It was too late – he was out of the door.

We could still hear the harp screaming, 'Master, master.'

'Go and bring them both back,' I shouted.

G ran out of the house and I followed. Will was racing further down the winding road, towards the cloud at the end of the way.

'Kill him if you have to.'

The harp screamed louder and louder. We ran, but our legs were heavy as we tried to keep up and he was a fast 'un, him. Will jumped through the cloud. G followed.

'You stay here, Matilda,' G said to me. 'I'll be back with them both, don't you worry.'

I stayed on the edge of the cloud to see what was happening. Will was nearly at the bottom of the marigold, my dear G just behind him. Soon all three would be back home with me.

Instead, I waited at the edge of that cloud for many months and nights. And now I sit at the end of the winding road, waiting till another comes and seals their innocence with mine.

WHISKY CHASERS
Peter Bunzl

Samir loves Joe's face. He studies it every day in class: a face as old as his own but already, in eighteen years, the cliffs and hills and odd proportions of its geography have been shaped by life's weather. Samir likes to observe the ever-watchful green eyes, hidden in their shadowy alcoves over the flat nose and cheekbones, and the heavy brow that scrunches up with Joe's moods – all those sculptural planes could have been carved by Easter Islanders. Then there's the pout of his lips, the pucker of their concentration or the twist of their anger. But most of all, Samir examines the thoughts as they cross the wide-open landscape of the face. Tries hard to read their cloud shapes from the merest shadow.

In class Joe is quiet, watching, but outside with his friends, his voice is loud and gruff and the words come flowing fast as streams; and he laughs roaring, water-falling chuckles and shouts primal animal cries. Alone in a sun-splashed space he will practise his shadow-boxing, dancing with his silhouette against a wall and throwing combination punches, ducking, covering and weaving from the phantom jabs it flings back at him. He walks with a swagger, rolling his shoulders; and when he talks he throws his arms wide in wild gestures and listens beating time with a hand on a thigh or drumming the table with his fingers. He likes to tell everyone he's done it with girls, girls from other schools, girls from nightclubs, and women, older women, and a model off the telly. He probably has as well, or at least wants to. He probably wants them the way Samir wants him.

Girls are alien creatures to Samir, big slow languid things, round and doughy with breasts and hips, all udders and eyelashes. Not like Joe, with his skinny, sinewy body, whippet fast and beanpole thin. A boy with so much energy it snaps and crackles off him like static. Samir wants Joe for the truth he thinks he's missing. He wants the feel of him, his warm body under a hand, wants his heartbeat through soft cotton, his breath against a cheek. Even the name, he wants the name: J-O-E – those three oh-so-English letters. He wants those. They possess his mind like a song, a mantra, like the turn of the planet – everything revolves around Joe.

After school Samir works at the Co-op. Nothing revolves around the Co-op, except maybe the late-night drunks and the people who come in to buy multi-pack dog food. And Mr Habib, the Co-op manager, who makes Samir tie his hair back with an elastic band when he's on duty behind the till or when he's manning the cigarette counter. Sometimes, when the shop is empty, Mr Habib comes over and straightens Samir's name tag, with its one star, then he puts a heavy hand on each of Samir's arms and squeezes his non-existent biceps.

'There,' he'll say. 'Much smarter. You will move up the ranks!'

Fridays are the best days at the Co-op because they're when Joe comes in to buy his cigarettes. He doesn't look at Samir and

Samir tries not to look at him as he doesn't have his hair to hide behind (it's not that long really, when it's loose, just long enough to conceal his ears and his eyes).

This is what Joe says to Samir: 'Twenty B&H. Cheers, mate.' And Samir nods, takes his money and gives him his change and his cigarettes. They never acknowledge each other, even though they're in the same class at school.

Today, before Joe comes over, Samir sees him in one of those big curved mirrors that hangs above the drinks aisle. He is wearing a russet-coloured woollen jumper that's far too big and makes him look like a sad sack. When he thinks no one is looking he pulls a flat-faced bottle of whisky from a high shelf, lifts his jumper and tucks the bottle between his belly and his belt. He glances up and, seeing Samir watching in the mirror, licks his lips and rubs his belly. Samir smiles because it's almost like that children's game – can you do the two things at once?

On the way out Joe puts his coins on the counter and looks Samir straight in the eye. 'Twenty B&H. Cheers, mate.' It's a test. He wants to see what Samir will do. But Samir does nothing. Says nothing, just scrapes the money up as usual, checks it's correct and then hands Joe his box of twenty fags. Joe smiles and gives him a wink. 'Thanks, man.' He holds up an empty hand. 'And thanks for the five-finger discount.'

His shift over, Samir shelters outside the shop, watching the rain and thinking about Joe. He rubs his work shirt across his wet hair, but it doesn't seem to make any difference so he stuffs it in his bag. Water spurts through a hole in the awning, spattering the pavement beside him. It sounds like someone pissing. He puts an elbow on the fruit and veg stand: the metal's cold against his skin. He's glad to be alone with the rain; there's something calming about it. Inside the shop the strip lights flicker out, and Mr Habib comes to the door.

'Samir, you still here?'

'Yeah.'

Samir watches as the manager pulls down the shutters and locks them.

'Want a lift home?'

'No thanks. My sister's picking me up.'

'You're sure?'

'Yeah, I prefer to wait – fresh air.'

'Well, I'll wait with you then, till she arrives. Doesn't do for a young lad like you to be alone in the street.'

'You don't have to do that,' Samir tells him.

But Mr Habib doesn't listen, just stands closer, too close, and looks out at the rain. 'Some September we're having, eh? Nice weather for ducks!'

Samir used to accept lifts home from Mr Habib until once, when he was going for the gear stick, the manager put his hand on Samir's leg and left it there for too long. Afterwards, he claimed it was an accident, but Samir wasn't so sure.

The blast of a car horn wakes him from his thoughts. Ayesha – thank God! She pulls up opposite in her Datsun, music blaring, and Samir pushes past the manager and runs across the street. He opens the passenger door and jumps in, popping the lock behind him. 'Come on, Ayesh. Let's go!' he says, as he yanks at the seat belt.

'OK, Sami, give me a second.'

The heaters are blasting out, along with her Bhangra tunes, and she nods her head in time to the beat as she leans over, opens the glove box, and feels about for her packet of cigarettes. When she finds them she flips the lid and pulls one out. Then she presses the car lighter, puts the gear stick into first and bunny-hops them down the street.

'We're back!' Samir calls out as he opens the front door. He hangs his coat on the banisters. Light spills from the landing, but the house is silent. In the kitchen the plates from breakfast are stacked in the sink. 'She's not here.'

Ayesha pushes past him and dumps her handbag on the sideboard among the piles of unopened mail. 'Probably gone to bed,' she says.

'Never got up, more like.' Samir slumps into a chair and kicks his legs out under the table.

Ayesha opens the fridge and takes out a bottle of lemonade. She pours herself a tall glass. 'Want one?'

He nods and she pulls a mug from the rubble of crockery, dribbles the dregs into it and hands it to him.

'Why don't I get a glass?'

'There aren't any.'

He sips the lemonade from the mug and pulls a face. 'Yuck. It tastes flat-rank.'

'What do you expect? It's been in there all week. Could probably do with a bit of something to pep it up. Bit of vodka, maybe.'

'Ayesha!'

'What? I'm only saying.'

Samir puts the mug down and pushes it away across the table. 'Why haven't you done the washing-up?' he asks.

'Wasn't my turn. You're supposed to do it.'

'We're supposed to be making life easier for her.'

'Whatever. You're such a suck-up.' Ayesha sits down opposite him and flicks through an old magazine. 'Besides, I did it yesterday.'

When Ayesha's gone to bed Samir ignores the washing-up. Instead he opens her bag and steals two cigarettes – Marlboro Lights. He puts one in his jacket pocket and the other he lights with a match from the box of Swan Vestas in the everything-drawer. He unlocks the back door and sits there trying to smoke. The smell reminds him of his dad, before he quit – quit the town, the country, them.

He takes a long wet drag on the cigarette, sucking in the smoke, gulping it down into his lungs. It tastes hot and scratchy, makes him cough, and he thinks he's going to retch, but he carries on anyway – that's what Joe would do.

A few more puffs and he gets up and bows his head over the sink. It feels like he's going to vomit, but nothing comes out except spittle. He takes a deep breath, and then another, and after a while he begins to feel better, not so light-headed. It's a disgusting business, this smoking, with practice he might get used to it.

On his way up to bed he checks on his mum. She's fallen asleep on top of the covers again, surrounded by piles of unsorted washing. His mother is wearing a cotton nightie with flowers round the neck. He's not seen it before and decides it must be an old one. Her hair straggles across the pillow in rats tails and she snores softly to herself and turns away from the light, alone in her dream world. He closes the door and leaves her to it.

The next day is Saturday. After he gets off his shift at the shop, Samir goes down to the wasteland. To the pond. It's not his place, but he knows it's where Joe goes – where everyone goes, to drink and smoke and do whatever. But, of course, no one's there now, because the sky is still light and those things can only happen after dark.

Samir walks down to the little shore where the wasteland meets the water. The mud splatters round the soles of his black shoes. He takes them off, and his socks too, and stands stretching his toes in the gloop. He likes the feel of it, his bare feet on the land, like his ancestors. There are ridged pie-crust pieces on the surface of the squidge. He presses at them with a toe.

In the pond carp and goldfish sweep about in muscular arcs of movement. He takes an old sandwich crust from his pocket and throws a few breadcrumbs to them. The fish brush against the watery roof of their world, their slick dark mouths breaking the surface to gulp down the bread pellets until, with a plop, they retreat into the shadowy depths.

There's a snap of twigs behind him and he turns to see Joe appear through a line of trees, ambling along. Joe stops momentarily when he realizes he's not alone but then, seeing who it is, he smiles and walks towards Samir.

'You again. What you doing?'

'Nothing.'

'Where are your shoes?'

'I don't need them.'

'Why not?'

'I like how the mud feels, that's all.' It sounds foolish out loud.

Joe looks at him as if he's crazy, then brushes past, feigning to step on his toes, but instead he hops along the waterline and stops a few feet away. Standing with the tips of his white trainers in the shallows, he taps out rings into the water and watches them as they spread and disappear.

Samir stares at the back of his head. His short clipped wheat-coloured hair – the crown a crop circle with tufts and the neckline a downy whorl of thin threads.

Joe scratches his neck, as if he can feel Samir's gaze.

Beside him a dead finch floats at the pond's edge, washing back and forth between the land and the water. Its neck broken, the head twisted round unnaturally, the wings stuck in mid-glide and the body bloated. Joe nudges it with the toe of his trainer.

'It's alive!'

'You're moving it.'

'I'm not, I swear. We should fish it out, chuck it somewhere – see if it flies.'

'Just leave it. It's dead.'

Joe takes the bottle of whisky from his pocket. It's half-drunk and the remaining amber liquid sloshes around inside it. He unscrews the cap and puts the bottle to his lips, tips his head back and takes a huge glug, then splutters, gasps and wipes a hand across his face. He offers the bottle to Samir, laughing.

'You wanna suck on the Devil's dick?'

'What?'

'Want some whisky? I owe you some.'

Samir thrusts his hands deep into his pockets. 'I can't.'

It's getting dark and Samir is walking with Joe. He's no idea where they're going. He's drunk and his head is filled with stars. Someone has opened up his skull and poured them in. And over there, behind the row of terraced houses, the moon is rising, the thinnest curviest crescent of a moon, and the streetlights stretch his shadow as Joe throws the empty whisky bottle into the road and it lands with a splintering smash of glass. Now Joe rings a doorbell and they go into a house. And now they're at a party. A house party.

They throw their coats on the pile at the foot of the stairs and wander down the dark hallway. The dull thump of drum and bass makes the floor shake and Samir's eardrums hum.

In the sitting room the furniture has been pushed to the walls and the expanse of carpet is filled with people, not dancing, but sitting cross-legged on the floor in little groups of twos and threes with their backs to each other, drinking cans of lager or alcopops, and smoking, they're all smoking, sucking on fire and breathing out dense grey fog.

Joe looks around, speaks to people: 'All right? What's up?'

He spots his mates and makes towards them. Samir steps over the sea of legs, following. There's a tink of metal and a 'Watch it!' and he looks down to see a boy holding a can out of his way.

'You almost had it over. Look next time, yeah?'

'Sorry,' he mumbles and looks about for Joe.

He's already sitting in his group. Samir walks over and squeezes himself in among them. To Joe's left is a rat-faced boy called Mark and on his other side is Chloe from school, with her big dangly earrings.

'You brought anything?' she asks Joe.

'Yeah,' he says, getting out his gear. 'You got any skins?'

She hands him a packet of Rizlas and he pulls out three papers, licks and sticks them together and tears off the excess. He burns the lighter under the dark brown hash and a thin line of smoke, sweet and acrid, wafts up from it. 'Mmm. Moroccan,' he says, crumbling some into the paper. 'Anyone got a spare fag?'

'Here you go.' Samir takes out his second cigarette, the one he stole from Ayesha, and proffers it to Joe.

'Thanks, bro. I didn't know you smoked.'

'Sometimes.'

Joe rolls the cigarette between his thumb and finger and tobacco falls from the end, tumbling into the Rizlas.

'Using the patented Mark method, I see,' Mark says, sipping from his can of Guinness.

'No, I'm using my method,' Joe says. 'I don't know how you can drink that stuff. It's disgusting.'

'I love it. Don't drink anything else.'

'What's it taste of?' Samir asks.

'It's gross,' Chloe says.

'Have you not tried it? You want some?' Mark offers him the can.

He takes it and knocks back a slug. It tastes malty and cold. Heavy. Not fiery like the whisky. 'It's OK,' he says, wiping a hand across his face.

'It's an acquired taste,' Mark says.

Chloe laughs. '"Acquired taste" – where d'you learn that one? Down the wine shop?'

'All right, all right. Shut up.' Mark turns to Samir. 'Did you not bring any beers of your own, mate?'

'No.'

'Here, try this.' Chloe picks up a spare open can.

Joe looks up from rolling his joint. 'Don't give him that one.'

'Why not?' Chloe asks. 'He wants some beer, don't you, Samir?' She offers him the can.

'Thanks.' Samir takes it cautiously and sips. It's almost full, tastes pretty good.

Joe picks up his joint and twirls the end between his fingers, making a white origami torpedo. 'Look at that – pure craftsmanship!'

'Should be, the amount of time it takes you to roll,' Mark says.

'Shut up.' Joe bites the paper tail off the joint with his teeth and lights the end with a Bic set to flame-thrower. He takes one long drag and lets it out slowly. 'Ah, that's the stuff.'

Samir takes another swig of beer. Suddenly he's very thirsty. He drinks fast, gulping down mouthfuls, until he notices the eyes of the group on him. A few more gulps and he realizes why – there's a cigarette butt in the can. It plunks around the top, grazes his teeth. Beer dribbles down his chin, he tries to close his mouth but now the butt's in his throat. He puts the can down. Leaves it. They all watch, waiting for him to pull a face or spit back into the can. He doesn't. Instead he gulps, swallowing the butt.

It tastes ashy – or is that his imagination. The thought of it turns his stomach and makes him retch. He takes a deep breath.

'How's the beer?' Chloe asks. 'Better than Guinness?'

Mark giggles. 'You should never minesweep. Did no one teach you that?'

Samir doesn't say anything. He won't give them the satisfaction. The bastards. After a moment, Joe puts a hand on his back.

'You all right?' he asks, exhaling smoke from his nose.

Samir nods. The others are waiting for the joint, but Joe leans over and passes it to him.

'Here you go, man. You deserve this.'

Minutes pass, or hours. The air is warm and treacly and things soften into each other, slow as a record played on the wrong setting. Someone rolls another joint and more people come and join them, sit and smoke, then leave. Samir drinks another can of beer that Joe gives him. He has to pull the ring this time, so he knows it's safe. Everything becomes hazy, with sudden puffs of detail like looking through smeared glasses. The feathery hairs on Joe's arm, the frayed ends of his own cuffs, mud caked on Mark's shoes, the dark roots of Chloe's hair and, when she tips her head forward, the swing of her hoop earrings. Birds could perch right on those earrings – dead birds, like the one in the pond. Stuffed birds. Stuffed dead-bird earrings. He smiles at the thought of such a thing, and the smile feels good, his cheeks moving the big mountainous landscape of his face. This makes him laugh even more and he can't stop the laughter, tries to stifle it like a sneeze, but it gathers, keeps on coming, bubbling up from the warmth of his belly until it overflows in an endless stream.

And now everyone's laughing at him laughing and his ribs ache with the effort of stopping and Joe smiles at him and an energy flows between them – not the high nervous energy he normally feels with people, but a deep warm slow energy, a low resonating bass note – or maybe that's the music. It has mellowed too and suddenly sounds really good.

Chloe comes back from the kitchen, Samir hadn't remembered her leaving. She puts one hand on a hip and sways slightly. 'We've only gone and run out of booze.'

Joe giggles. 'Someone's going to have to do an offie run.'

'By someone I s'pose you mean me?' Mark says.

'Hey, don't worry,' Chloe says. 'We'll come too.'

Joe shrugs. 'Whatever. Be good to get some air.' He stands slowly and unsteadily on his feet. 'Come on, all of you.'

Mark is driving. His car is even crumbier than Ayesha's. Chloe sits beside him in the front seat and Samir sits in the back, next to Joe, their legs touching. He winds down the window. After the fug of the smoke-filled room the air tastes good again

– dark and cold as blueberry ice cream. Outside the dead town coasts past, 3 a.m. quiet.

Chloe finds a torch in the car's glove compartment and shines it out the window at the countryside streaming past. Samir watches as the light picks out the treetops; the leaves look alien in the soft dim circle of yellow.

Now Chloe flicks the torch into the car.

'Fuck!' Mark says. 'Quit shining that on me.'

'OK, OK.' She turns and shines the torch on Samir. 'How you doing back there, Sam, mate?'

'Fine.'

'Don't speak much, do you?'

'S'pose not.'

'See anyone you liked at the party?'

'No.'

She pushes the torch at him. Shines it in his eyes. 'Really?'

'Leave him alone,' Joe says.

'Why?' She turns the light on him creating a burnt-out ring of white across his face. 'I'm talking to Sam, not you, wanker.'

'You're so boring when you're drunk, Chloe.'

'And you're boring when I'm sober.'

'Stop waving that thing about, will you? You'll cause a fucking accident.' Joe grabs the torch from her and turns it off. Now there's just the darkness of the car and the headlights on the road. He points out a derelict pub as they fly past. 'That's where Mum used to work.'

'I bet it's where she met that idiot,' Chloe says. 'You were probably conceived in the ladies' toilets. Right there on the seat.'

Samir glances over at the pub. The Bricklayer's Arms. He went in there with his dad once, years ago. It was their secret. Was Joe's mum working that day? They'd played the fruit machine and it had gurgled like a greedy baby, trilling and flashing blue and pink when he'd put the money in. He'd pulled the lever and got three bells and a rush of coins had tumbled into the dish. Wide-eyed, he'd scooped them up, his dad laughing. 'Beginner's luck.'

The off-licence is shut. The windows dark behind the bolted security grills.

'I thought it never closed,' Joe says. 'Isn't it supposed to be twenty-four hours?'

'Are off-licences ever really twenty-four hours?' Chloe asks.

Mark drums his fingers on the steering wheel, thinking. 'I've got it!' he says. 'Maybe we've entered the twilight zone and this is the twenty-fifth hour.'

'Could be.' Chloe presses the car's lighter and when the button finally pops she lights a cigarette with the red hot filament and takes a long drag.

'We could go to the Co-op instead,' she says at last.

Samir shakes his head. 'It's closed.'

'Yeah, but you've got the spare keys, haven't you?'

'Have you?' Joe asks.

'How did you know that?' Samir asks her.

'I used to work there, remember?' She turns to Joe. 'They always give you a spare key if you have to open up Saturday mornings. They'll have given it to him. They bloody love him there, don't they, Samir?'

'Cool,' Mark says. 'Let's go there, then.'

'It's breaking and entering,' Samir says.

'Not if you're with us,' Joe tells him. 'Don't worry. We'll pay for the booze.'

'How?'

'We'll give you the money and you can put it in the till for us when you're next in.'

Samir hooks a loose lock of hair behind his ear. 'That's not a good idea,' he says.

'You don't have to come with us.' Joe puts a hand gently on Samir's shoulder. 'We just need the keys, that's all.'

'Yeah. Don't come with us,' Chloe says, laughing. 'You can walk back.'

They pull up down the street from the Co-op and stare at the heavy metal shutters, graffitied with purple tags.

Samir rubs a streak of cigarette ash from the front of his jeans. A nagging knot of fear is developing in his chest. 'I'm not opening the shop,' he says. 'We can go round the back, through the stockroom.'

'The stockroom'll be fine.' Joe leans over and musses his hair until it falls about his face. 'Thanks for doing this, Samir.' He turns to the others. 'Chloe, Mark, you'd better wait in the car, make sure no one sees us.'

Crouching behind the dustbins, Samir fiddles with the heavy-duty lock on the Co-op's back door. Joe stands beside him, keeping a lookout. It takes a minute for the lock to give because it's so stiff, but finally it releases with a click and he pulls the door open a crack so he and Joe can duck inside.

The stockroom alarm panel, screwed to the breeze-block wall, bleeps out a warning. Samir walks over and turns its key, which is always in there, to the off position. And now there's just the silence and the sharp smell of disinfectant that fills the closed room.

Joe holds the torch by his side so that the light falls along his leg and leaves a soft yellow circle on the grit-covered linoleum. Leading him round the towers of stacked boxes, Samir almost bangs his hip on the handle of a loading trolley. They pass a chest freezer filled with frosty, plastic covered meat and stop in front of a row of metal shelves stacked with liquor and cans.

'Let's just get a couple of bottles of spirits,' Joe says. Standing on tiptoe, he leans forward, his chest level with Samir's face.

He's reaching for the expensive stuff, grabbing at a bottle of whisky on a high shelf. It totters, rocking back and forth.

'Careful,' Samir says.

Joe's fingers grasp for the bottle again. It topples and, as it falls, he jumps back, his body brushing against Samir's, their belt buckles scraping together.

The bottle smashes on the floor, spraying glass and whisky everywhere. Joe drops the torch, and there's a plastic crack and they are plunged into darkness.

'Shit,' he whispers. 'That was close. I thought we were going to get hit by flying glass.' He's holding on to Samir, leaning into him, and Samir can feel Joe's heartbeat in his own chest.

Joe takes the Bic from his pocket. Holding it up, he flicks the wheel, and there's a tiny flinty spark, like the dying blink of a firework, that seems to hang in the air for a moment between them, but no flame.

'It's broken.' Joe shakes the lighter violently and turns it up to full blast, and now the flame jumps tall, illuminating his face, and his eyes shine out bright as a cat's. 'It works!' He laughs, but it goes out again.

'Man, I'm too stoned for this.'

'Give me your hand,' Samir says.

His eyesight is adjusting to the dark and his senses are intensified. He reaches out and takes one of Joe's hands and an electric frisson passes between them. Samir's heart beats faster, pulsing in his mouth, making his whole body shake; Joe's breath is warm on his face, his palm coarse and dry. If he's going to do it, it must be now. Now is the moment. Slowly, he leans in and kisses Joe's cheek and then the soft warmth of his lips. And in the space of a breath Joe kisses him back.

It's a good kiss. His first. Light and sugary soft, with a smoky aftertaste. But it only lasts an instant and then Joe pulls away and gives a high nervous giggle. And the moment's gone, broken in two. So brief that afterwards Samir thinks he must have imagined it, and yet he's shaking, and his fingers can still feel the pressure of the grasp so quickly pulled away.

'Man, I'm stoned,' Joe mumbles.

'Me too,' Samir says, but he doesn't feel it. All of a sudden he feels completely sober.

Joe touches his shoulder lightly and reaches up to take another bottle of whisky off the shelf. 'Come on,' he says. 'We'd best be going.'

Samir steps over the broken mess of glass on the floor. He'll have to clear it up tomorrow. As they approach the exit a sliver of light breaks through from the yard.

Outside it has started to rain again, another downpour. They run towards the car and Chloe leans over and pulls up the tab to open the door for them. She's sitting in the back now and Joe hands her the whisky bottle and climbs in beside her. Spreading himself across the seat he nuzzles her neck. She laughs and tries to push him away. 'Get off!' she shrieks as he sprawls all over her.

There's no room for Samir on the backseat so he sits up front with Mark. They drive off and Mark and Chloe won't stop talking. They must have taken something else while Samir and Joe were in the shop. Samir looks to Joe, but Joe won't meet his gaze.

'A light came on at the upstairs window,' Mark tells them excitedly, 'right above the shop. And then a car drove past and a van, and we had to duck down and pretend we weren't there, didn't we, Chloe?'

'Yeah,' she says, 'and then we heard some shouting up the road and a dog barking and all sorts. And you were both taking so long, we thought something must have happened to you. Did something happen to you?' she asks Joe.

The words fill the darkness of the car. Joe answers without looking up. 'Nothing happened to us,' he says, a little too loudly. 'Isn't that right, Samir?'

Samir nods and agrees that nothing happened.

***

Five minutes later they're in the countryside, flying along the narrow lanes in silence. Mark is driving too fast. Samir's head feels heavy and his hands, clasped in his lap, will not keep still, his fingers twined together won't stop shaking.

On the back seat Joe and Chloe are necking. He tries not to look but he keeps catching glimpses of them in the mirror, their framed reflections flashing in the passing beams of light. Chloe's hair is loose and her hoop earrings swing back and forth with the bounce of the car. Joe bends forwards and puts a hand under her blouse, and the collar of his jacket rides up the back of his neck. Suddenly Samir wishes he was anywhere but here with these people.

Outside the window a row of trees strobes past. They look like the silhouettes of figures. Giant shadow men who could jump into the road and flip the car over, crack the glass into spider's webs with their large fists. A bird flaps by Samir's window, scared up from the dark verges. And as the lane narrows two headlights come towards them. Full on. Joe and Chloe break off kissing, their eyes wide as the approaching lamps.

'What's that?' Joe asks.

Samir opens his mouth to answer, but his words are drowned out by the streaking scream of a car horn.

THE UNICORN
Paul Yates

'I think Miss Danes is a racist, quizzing me on precisely where and when, and "Do you have your parents' permission to travel to Paris alone?" I told her I wouldn't be alone, I'd be with you. She just looked at me sideways and gave one of her frowns. It's because I'm an Arab. She didn't ask you anything, did she?'

'That's all nonsense, Fariza. You know she doesn't give a fuck about the English girls. It's because your parents are thousands of miles away and the school is responsible for you and needs your dad's money.'

'Huh, you wouldn't think I paid her wages the way she talks to me. And if they were really concerned they wouldn't let me go with you, would they, Alice?'

Alice turned to look at her friend.

'That's... sometimes you are simply absurd.'

Fariza and Alice sat together on a scruffy sofa in the sixth-form common room, empty now that most girls had left for half term.

'Finish your coffee, kid. We'd better get a move on. We don't want to miss the TGV. Are you packed?'

'Sort of. It's good to be wearing proper clothes,' Fariza said.

She stood up and smoothed out the wrinkles in a short red skirt with a slim brown hand. Delicately, she eased her knickers out of the cleavage of her buttocks.

'Come on, then,' she said, and pulled at the tops of her pirate boots, which slid down immediately on their release.

They clattered up the uncarpeted wooden staircase to the study bedroom they shared.

'My God, it's so cold in here,' Fariza said, rubbing her palms together. 'They've turned the heating off and we haven't even left yet.'

Outside, a freezing wind blew stinging sleet into their faces from a February sky pregnant with snow. Heads down, they ran across the bleak courtyard, the wheels of their cabin bags bouncing on the cobbles behind them.

At the porters' lodge they signed out with Mr Galley, who ordered them a taxi for Brighton station. Alice, as her mother had instructed her, slipped him a banknote, as she did every half-term and double at Christmas. It made him amenable to the occasional errand in town, even cigarettes, though he'd drawn the line at vodka when Fariza had put her up to it. As he'd accurately observed, it was more than his job was worth.

At the station Fariza dived into M&S and bought sandwiches, crisps and drinks. They worked their way through them as the train wound slowly through south-east London to St Pancras.

Every other person on the concourse seemed to be carrying skis.

'I tried it on the dry slopes in Dubai,' Fariza said, 'but it's crap, and I knew this girl who was only our age and she'd totally fucked her knees.'

'It can be fun,' Alice said, 'but it depends entirely who you're with.'

Alice paused at the statue of John Betjeman. 'My grandad

says he was a great Englishman, even if he was a poet, but he looks gaga to me.'

Fariza snorted. 'Shall I see if I can get us bumped up?'

'It's a train, Fariza – forget it,' Alice said. 'Anyway, the people in first class are ghastly and the champagne's piss.'

'Wicked,' Fariza said, and returned to sucking the thin violet straw that gave her access to the bottom layers of her third cocktail, 'and they're so pretty.'

'Can we afford this?' Alice asked.

'Of course. I'm hungry, let's eat,' Fariza said, sliding from her bar stool.

The restaurant was still dressed for autumn, embellished with wheat sheaves and agricultural artefacts rendered in a range of pale greys and browns.

'It's a shame,' Alice said, 'the French aren't sentimental about the countryside, unlike the bloody English. For them it's where you go to kill things. I guess this is for Americans, like our sunken pulsating bath.'

'And Arabs,' Fariza said.

The food was like that in any other international hotel, only in French. Expensively packaged, meticulously served and dull.

'I've got a little confession to make,' Fariza said over coffee. 'I've got a special reason to be here.'

'Oh, my God. Don't tell me.'

'Remember I said I'd met this boy, Amer, at a party in Amman at Christmas? The Lebanese guy who lives in Tangier and is absolutely gorgeous? He's come to his auntie's in Paris to fetch me and we're going over to meet his family.'

'In Tangier?'

'Yes, it's not very far. He wants to marry me. I know English girls aren't at all romantic about marriage, but we are.'

'You are not romantic, Fariza. You think men are meat and you rate them by their arse factor. What about a visa?'

'Did it by post during term. He's the right sort of guy, not macho, not religious, good arse –' she looked at her friend – 'and if his family is halfway decent it's probably worth a try. Could save years of hassle with my parents.'

Alice closed her eyes and let her head fall backward.

'You're fucking nuts, Fariza. People don't get married at eighteen, not even crazy ones like you.'

'Some Muslim girls marry at fourteen.'

'So you want to make up for lost time?'

'I'll only be gone forty-eight hours max. Back for dinner Sunday – promise. I'm sorry, I should have told you.'

'You were quite right not to. If I'd known, I wouldn't have given you cover.'

'Best friends?' Fariza said, putting her head on one side and looking at Alice from under long black lashes.

Alice stretched her hand across the table and put it over Fariza's.

'I think you've lost it. Your parents will go bananas – even mine would. Just shag him if that's what you want. Now, repeat after me – "Marriage is just bloody servitude, with diminishing sexual returns and no remission for good behaviour." Got it, sister?'

Alice got up and gripped the back of her chair, leaning towards Fariza.

'I'm going to the bar. If you think you can be remotely sensible, join me.'

Fariza followed Alice. She pushed her bare shoulders down, tucked her bra straps under the ribbons that held up her black silk dress and tilted her pelvis.

'You're not being fair,' Fariza said, and pouted. 'You know I can't just shag him at his auntie's.'

'Then bring him back here and I'll go into a Young Women's Christian Association hostel for the night. I've been confirmed.'

They sat in a corner of the dimly lit bar with large vodkas.

'What a giveaway,' Alice said, raising her glass. 'Only English schoolgirls drink vodka.'

'I don't know what to do now. I thought you might see it as an adventure, that you'd support me. I think I'll have to go – it'll be fine.'

'You know what I think and I guess it's up to you. Just keep in touch and make sure you get back on time.'

Alice finally gave in to bladder pressure and went for a wee. She looked at her watch: 5.30. Outside, the revolving light on the Eiffel Tower fitfully lit up the cemetery on the other side of the road. Snow covered the roofs of the tiny chapels coating the graves and the narrow walkways. The black tracks of feral cats added to the general Gothic atmosphere. She picked up a note from Fariza's pillow and read it on the loo.

> Back in 48hrs
> have fun. C U soon.
> Love you lots.
> F xxxx

Alice groaned, feeling slightly nauseous. She took some painkillers and went back to bed.

In the breakfast room a young cook with blond curls was piling up brioches, dainty miniature pains au raisin and flaky crescents of buttery croissants. He looked familiar and rather nice in tight whites. Alice looked at his bum. Fariza was right, it was so often a man's best feature, but it was way too early to even think about it.

'Hi, you're Alice, aren't you? Jamie – Jamie Cullingford. I would shake hands, but it's probably frowned upon.'

'Wow – you're a bit of a surprise,' Alice said. 'Haven't seen you since Sam's appalling summer do, where, as I recall, you were getting rat-arsed for England.'

'Young and foolish, I'm afraid. But look at me now – an honest artisan patissier. Hey, I'm off at eleven – how about coffee?'

'Yeah, that'll be great.'

He lowered his voice. 'They don't like fraternization, so meet me on the corner of Rue Lepic.'

The maître d' approached Alice.

'*Pour une personne, madame?*'

'*Oui.*'

She winked at Jamie and followed the immaculate penguin to a small table by the window. Alice sat down, looked up into the eyes of the unsmiling man and smiled.

'*Bonjour, Monsieur. Café et oeufs brouillés pour moi, s'il vous plaît. Chambre deux cent huit.*'

'Good morning. Of course, madam, thank you,' he said, and returned the smile.

The buggers always do that in Paris. It's like you're a stick of rock with 'English' written all through it. Still, better than down south, where they just stare at you, like you're an imbecile, or worse, ignore you. Alice liked Paris. It was cosier than London, but it had drawbacks. She stared out of the window at the chilled Parisians making their way to work, or somewhere.

'Durham was cold, not as cold as this, and in the Dark Ages. It's got ninety-three restaurants and they're all Italian and crap. Got a lousy degree, waste of my golden youth, really,' Jamie said. 'Parents needed to get rid of me – made me do a load of aptitude tests – I like making clay models so I came out as a baker – artisan bakers are all the go – didn't want to make bread that doubles as hardcore – so patisserie and Paris. I get bed and pocket money – they get a slave.'

'Thanks, Jamie. I only asked how's it going. You sure you're not confusing me with your official biographer?'

A waitress brought their coffees and set down two small glasses of chilled water.

'I don't want to go to uni. It sounds worse than school. Essays and exams and full of pimply boys who come if you look at them – vomit. Given I now know all, Jamie, once fledged as a baker, *à la ponce*, where do you fly to?'

'London, of course. Cadge the money for a bakery, do some pop-ups and markets and, when I've got me a stash, open a shop in Kensington village, next door to Ottolenghi. Do you want to get in on the ground floor?'

Alice sipped from her glass.

'Why do they serve iced water with coffee, when the temperature is twenty below?'

'Lots of places don't bother. It's old school.' He paused. 'I mean it, you know.'

'I'm sure you do, and it's entirely laudable, but I don't have stacks of ready at the moment. Let's go. I need to smoke,' Alice said, getting up and grabbing her bag.

They stood in the street as people and traffic pulsed round them, each absorbed in the romance of smoking. Alice took her cigarette out of her mouth and looked at it between long, face-disfiguring draws. She checked her phone and returned it to her bag, zipping it into an inside compartment.

Jamie flicked his cigarette butt into the gutter and thrust his hands into the pockets of his jeans.

'I'm off to Cluny,' Alice said. 'Do you want to come?'

'Bit of a trek. What's there?'

'Unicorns, of course, and ghosts of Romans.'

The two-storey house was set in an orchard of scrub, dotted with lemon, fig and pomegranate trees. It was built of wood and stone. Old vines clung to the walls. Wide double doors led into an inner courtyard, shaded by a tall palm in the centre. A staircase mounted to an arcade that ran around three sides. In one corner stood a masonry well-head with a rusting iron cap.

It was old; no one Fariza knew lived in an old house. Some steps led to a door that opened directly on to a large salon. Small, screened windows threw patterns of light on to the rugs and flagstones that covered the floor. Furniture, arranged around the walls, was sparse and dark. There was a sweet smell of scented tobacco.

As her eyes became accustomed to the light, Fariza saw that some of the chairs were occupied. A thin man in a grey suit got up and advanced towards them. He shook Amer's hand and bowed briefly to Fariza, welcoming them in heavily accented Arabic. With a sweep of his hand he included three other men, all in dark suits, who sat in large chairs. They inclined their heads and smiled.

Amer led Fariza to the back of the house, where a group of women sat on sofas, drinking tea. Their talk stopped and they looked at the couple. All the women, and the little girls who sat on pouffes by them, were covered up, but in expensive Western clothes. Some, laden with traditional gold jewellery, jangled as they moved. Fariza pulled her scarf forward and tucked her hair in. The greeting was formal and they made little conversation. After a few moments Amer steered Fariza towards a staircase.

'I guess they all seem a bit old-fashioned to you,' he said, as he showed Fariza into a bedroom.

'I've got all sorts of relatives,' Fariza said. 'My Arabic's not brilliant and it's hard to understand what's being said.'

'You'll soon get used to it, don't worry. You unpack. I'll come and get you in a while and we'll have some tea.' He smiled, held her hand briefly and was gone.

Fariza put her case into an armoire in the corner of the room. She sat on the bed and looked around. The room was large and sparsely furnished. A double casement looked out on to the garden. Her hand rummaged in her bag, then she peered into it and got up, emptying the contents on to the bed. Her phone was not there.

'Fuck,' Fariza said. 'Fuck, fuck, fuck – I can't believe it.'

Amer returned to take her to tea. They went down the stairs and sat side by side in the salon.

'Listen, Amer, my phone's gone. I had it in the taxi, I texted Paris – but it's not there now.'

'That's terrible. But don't worry, we'll get a new one tomorrow.'

Two women came in and served mint tea in small painted glasses. They set a circular dish piled high with pale, spiced pastries on a low central table before returning to the back of the house. Amer put some on a plate and handed them to Fariza. She nibbled one. It was dry and the red cinnamon paste was overpowering. She put it back on the plate and sipped the warm sweet tea. No one spoke to her. The men sporadically addressed Amer in their impenetrable Arabic.

'They say it would be good to visit my parents' village in the country. They like you very much and think we could get married there.'

Fariza sat still and quiet for some time. Turning to Amer, she smiled and spoke softly.

'Did I get that right? Have you completely lost the fucking plot. I'm here to see and be seen. That's all. As far as I'm concerned, we're still a long way from marriage. My parents would go berserk. You'd better tell your uncles, right now, this isn't going to happen.'

Fariza got up and left the room. She sat bolt upright on her bed, staring out of the window as dusk gradually fell. She couldn't even borrow a phone as she could barely remember any numbers, they were all on her SIM.

Amer appeared in the doorway and stood, clasping and unclasping his hands.

'It's all right,' he said. 'It's not marriage, it's a kind of betrothal. They're only thinking of you. They want it done to protect you.'

Fariza jumped up and stood in front of him, her hands on her hips.

'Protect me,' she said, 'what from?'

Amer backed into the corridor before coming slowly forward into the room.

'You know, your honour and stuff – for your family.'

'We can do that for ourselves, thanks.'

'Look,' Amer said, 'if I don't do what they say, they'll make trouble for my mother. It's just a bit of tradition.' He turned to go. 'We'll eat when the sun's gone down. Think about it, please.' He smiled and was gone.

The entrance to the museum was in a side street, a small door set in a long wall. Inside, they were immediately surrounded by the vast portable treasures of the medieval church.

'Have you got any dope?' Alice asked.

'Nope. It wouldn't go with getting up at four to make the morning goods. When I get time off, I sleep.'

'It's in here,' Alice said, and led Jamie into a barely lit, circular, chapel-like space hung with a series of six large, fifteenth-century tapestries of stylized woodland. Prominently featured in each, elegant heraldic unicorns disported in fields of embroidered flowers. A few people stood admiring them; no one spoke.

'I was about eight when I first came here. I fell in love with the unicorns – and if you try a Freudian joke, you're dead meat. More than anything, I wanted to be a unicorn and live in the tapestry. I've never desired anything quite so much. They were incredibly strong and could never be captured, only tamed by a young maid.' She turned to look at Jamie. 'There are pictures of the Virgin Mary with a unicorn. Perhaps I'll have to write a novel about them.'

'Give you a break from vampires and werewolves,' Jamie said.

They sat on a stone bench, in front of the elegantly restored remains of a Roman bathhouse. Alice's phone bleeped. It was from a boy who imagined he had a claim on her affections.

> I miss u so much.
> Send me a selfie of ur tits now.
> Please please please.

It was the work of moments for Alice to text back:

> Fuck off. Wanker.

She replaced the phone in her bag. It bleeped again. She ignored it.

'The other thing I have to do is vespers at Sacré-Coeur. You sing along with the convent choir. Sounds poncey, but it's better than Glasto and no mud.'

'I'll take your word for it. I think I might prefer the mud. I'll have to get back to work soon, but what about supper tomorrow? If your mate what's-her-name's back she can join us.'

'Sounds great.'

'There's a little family-run Lebanese I go to by Abbesse. Good nosh and affordable. I'll book now,' Jamie said, and got out his phone.

Alice reached for hers. There was a text from Fariza.

> He's gorgeous. On my way to meet dodgy uncles.
> Everyone talks weird Arabic here.
> Text when I can. ETA CDG 18.00 Sun.
> Love you. F xxxxxx

'That was Fariza,' Alice said. 'She'll be back for supper tomorrow. I'm off to the Palais-Royal to buy some ultra-expensive chocs.'

They parted in the street. Jamie held Alice's upper arm and kissed her cheek.

'*Au 'voir*,' he said.

* * *

After vespers, as Alice got up to leave, some young men came into the nave and one of them was using a flash on his phone. Immediately, they were surrounded by ushers, who shouted at them and pointed fingers in accusation. The crowd froze and moved away, isolating the culprits, as the ushers bundled them out of the basilica. Outside, chatting and giggling, the nuns from the choir were threading their way in pairs across the cobbles to their nunnery.

Wrapping her arms around herself against the cold, Alice headed back to the hotel, wondering why she had heard nothing further from Fariza. She didn't fancy a restaurant on her own and so stopped at a 8 à Huit and picked up a bottle of vodka. At the hotel she ordered supper in her room and a bucket of ice. She tried to phone but only got 'not available' in Arabic. So, Fariza was still in Tangier. Alice put on the telly and searched for the film channel.

'I don't quite get it,' Fariza said. She sidestepped a wizened beggar woman who sat on her haunches, eyes on the ground, clutching a grimy plastic cup. 'I should have been eating with the women, asking me my line on breastfeeding and measuring my hips.'

Amer and Fariza emerged into a large square. At one end domed minarets glowed in the sunlight. Shoppers and tourists milled around the shops, cafés and stalls that filled the space.

'I think my aunties and cousins are just a bit shy,' he said, leading her across the square. He stopped and looked around. 'The phone shop is here somewhere. You know, my uncles really want you to visit the village, but it'll have to be Monday morning. They've got you a new reservation for the afternoon. I'm sure your friend won't mind – you'll only be few hours late.'

Fariza stopped and swung round. She grabbed Amer by the lapels of his jacket.

'You've done fucking what?' She put her face just a few centimetres from his. 'Without asking me! What the fuck is going on?'

Amer stepped back and stuck his hands in his pockets.

'I guess things are a bit more traditional here, but then you could be, you know, sort of a bit more like an ordinary Muslim woman.'

'What,' Fariza shouted.

Some people stopped to look at them. Amer took her arm and started walking.

'I'm sorry. Everything will be all right. I can't see the phone shop – it used to be on this street, but perhaps it's closed. We could look for a stall that sells them in the market, but they'll only be refurbs. Let's stop for a coffee and calm down.'

Fariza sat with her face immobile, staring into the square. She did not look at Amer. Ignoring the tiny cup of syrupy coffee in front of her, she downed in one gulp the glass of arak she had insisted on ordering. The waiter had put the glass in front of Amer and had raised his eyebrows and one shoulder when Fariza immediately leaned over and took it.

Amer stood up and spread his hands in front of him.

'I'll take you back and then go to the market and try to find you a phone. Things will be fine, I promise. One other tiny thing. My uncles need your passport for some form to do with the betrothal.'

Fariza's mouth dried and her heart began to pound. With an effort she quelled the thought that she had no phone and nobody knew where she was. Amer smiled.

'Let's go anyway,' Alice said, as she put her phone away. 'People die if they don't eat. I'll leave a message with reception as her phone is kaput. At least we know the plane has landed.'

Jamie and Alice had been waiting in her room for Fariza. He had arrived via the service lift.

'Fine,' he said. 'I'll meet you on the corner. Don't be long, or I'll get frostbitten.'

'Don't worry, Jamie. I'll "put a girdle round about the earth".'

'What?'

'Forget it.'

In other circumstances Alice would have loved the restaurant. Small tables with paper tablecloths, napkins so flimsy one could see through them, lots of plastic flowers and cutlery that bent if one leaned on it. Also, despite Jamie's homely advertisement, prices to make one's eyes water. The food was excellent, fresh, tasty, plentiful and prettily served by rather lovely boys with kohl on their eyes; the Lebanese wines, fragrant and full.

Fariza failed to arrive and throughout the meal Alice was distracted. Jamie continually tried to be reassuring, saying that this or that might have delayed her.

'I'm sorry. I've been crap, Jamie. I'm anxious. Please, let me get the bill.'

Alice caught the waiter's eye, looked meaningful and made a scribbling motion on her palm.

'That's really kind, Alice. I bet she'll be at the hotel when we get back. She might have broken her ankle as well as losing her phone.'

They parted in the street and Jamie made his way via the staffs' permitted pathways to Alice's room.

'No messages, and the airline refuse to tell me whether she was on the plane, even when I said she was my sister and the whole family was worried about her. These people are shits. Vodka? I'll get some ice brought up.'

'I'm beginning to think there may be a problem,' Jamie said. 'If she was back in France I cannot think what would stop her getting in touch.'

'But if she's still in Tangier,' Alice said, 'she could go out and get a new phone, or she could borrow someone's, and surely the house will have a landline?'

There was a knock on the door. Jamie put a finger to his lips. Alice opened the door, took the ice bucket from the young waiter and gave him five euros.

'What the fuck am I going to do, Jamie?' Alice said. She sat on the bed clutching the ice bucket. 'I don't want to land her in trouble by going to the gendarmerie. They'll be really heavy. If I get the school involved there'll be a diplomatic incident. I don't know how to contact her parents. But I can't abandon her, she's my best mate. What if I've let her get kidnapped? Perhaps I should go to Tangier – but that's crazy.'

'What about this bloke she went to meet? Do you know where?'

'I think she said Saint-Denis, somewhere near the cathedral or the football stadium. But she didn't tell me the address. She did leave her case, though. Perhaps we should go through that?'

'Excellent idea.'

Alice slid back the mirror door of a closet and took out Fariza's pink Samsonite case. It wasn't locked. Inside was a jumble of tops, knickers, socks, a couple of dresses and a pair of black stilettos, along with a variety of scents and cosmetics. In a pocket in the lid was a scarlet Moleskine notebook. It was full of scribbles, jottings, lists, notes to do things and see people at school. Among these random items, decorated with hearts, was a name, Amer, with a Paris address:

Amer Mansur
entrée A no 6
38 rue saint-just
74001 Paris

'Thank God, Jamie, something concrete. We know where she went. I'll get over there tomorrow morning and see what I can find out.'

'Wait till breakfast is over and I'll come with you,' Jamie said.
'I feel involved now and I want to help you find her. Can I sleep here, in Fariza's bed? I've got to be in the kitchen in a few hours.'
'Sure, so long as you behave, got it?'
'Thanks, Alice. You won't know I'm here.'
'I will.'

Unable to sleep, Alice lay awake for a long time before lapsing into a fitful doze. She awoke to find Jamie next to her, his hand on her bum. She whipped round in the bed to face him.

'Fuck off, Jamie, I'm tired. What is this? Do you think if you don't try it on your willy will drop off? Get out of my bed. Good night, sleep well, and if you need to wank, do it in the corridor.'

Later, still unable to sleep, she relented. Jamie's artless athleticism failed to soothe, so she made him come as soon as was polite, and sent him back to Fariza's bed. Soon after she fell asleep. Jamie had been in the kitchen for four hours by the time she woke.

Hunched into their coats, they sat either side of a small round table on a café terrace. Alice had one hand round her rapidly cooling hot chocolate and a Gitane in the other. The patio heaters hissed above them.

'Whoever thought France would do this to people?' she said. 'My dad told me just a few years ago they were twenty cents a pack and everybody smoked, everywhere, all the time – imagine.'

'Drink your choco,' Jamie said. 'It'll be frappé in another thirty seconds. And I am sorry about last night, honest – I should have been more thoughtful.'

'Right! Fuck this,' Alice said. She stood up and ground her cigarette into the tiny blue ashtray. 'Let's get to Saint-Denis.'

Jamie pushed a note under the clip that held the bill on a small metal plate.

'Fine,' Jamie said. 'If we walk to Place de Clichy, we won't have to change on the Métro.'

They threaded their way down Rue Lepic, past the static knots of tourists entranced by the exotic fish stalls and enticing food shops.

'I hate tourists,' Alice said, 'but in a way I am one... What does that say about me?'

'Not a lot,' Jamie said.

They emerged from the Métro at Basilique into a grey suburb surreally dominated by a vast Gothic edifice. They found Rue Saint-Just behind the cathedral. Number 38 was a small apartment block. There was no concierge, or lift, and so they walked up to the third floor and found apartment 6. They were faced by a featureless door without a knocker or bell. Jamie rapped on it loudly. After a few moments the door was opened just enough for them to see a tall Arab man in a grey suit. He looked at them without smiling and said nothing.

'Good Morning, Monsieur. My name is Alice and I am a friend of Fariza. I believe she has been here recently.'

The man looked at Alice and then at Jamie. He spoke in rapid, accented French for some thirty seconds, then firmly closed the door. Alice immediately hammered on the wood with her fist. After a little while, when it was obvious she was not going away, the door opened a crack. Alice put all her weight against it and crashed into the apartment. The man fell back and Jamie followed her into an ill-lit passageway. The man held up his arms, palms outward.

'OK, OK, OK, what do you want? Explain to me again. Perhaps I misunderstood your French. Try to be calm, young lady.' He did not invite them into any room but stood blocking the hallway.

Alice repeated, in careful if Anglicized French, her enquiry after Fariza.

'It is possible she was here,' the man said. 'I have been abroad and am only lately returned. My wife has many nephews and may have entertained some young people, as you say. I do not know.

Unfortunately she has gone to Beirut to visit with her mother.'

'The boy's name is Amer and the girl was Fariza. Did your wife say anything about them at all to you before she went away?'

'I am afraid not, and her mother is not well, so she may be gone a month or more. You know how it is. I am very sorry that I am unable to be helpful, but I have no information.'

'Do you have an address or a phone number for Amer in Tangier?'

'My wife has many relations in Maroc. I really don't know.'

'Then can I have your wife's phone number please?'

'I am sorry but she does not carry a mobile and her mother lives in a village. And now perhaps you will leave me in peace,' the man said, and moved to open the door.

Alice almost ran down the stairs and stood on the pavement, fists clenched, looking up at what she took to be the windows of the flat.

'Do you know how to pick locks, Jamie?'

'Christ, Alice, cool it,' Jamie said. 'I don't know about that guy, but you sure scared the shit out of me. That was probably illegal, forced entry or some such thing.'

'What, and kidnapping isn't? He was lying through his fucking teeth.'

'But we do know she was there, and if we have to go to the police, they'll have somewhere to start from,' Jamie said.

'I think we should wait for him to go out and then break in somehow. There must be a fire escape.'

'First,' Jamie said, 'let's have a coffee and a ciggie at the café across the road and think about things, and then I have to get back for a big wedding breakfast. I'll see you as soon as I can after that.'

Fariza looked up to heaven. Thank God for Dad. Like her sisters, she had been born in Seattle at her uncle's house. Thus, as an American citizen, she held a US passport as well as a

Jordanian one. She always travelled with both and had given the US one to Amer. The Jordanian passport had the visa stamp for Morocco. She slipped a credit card and a bundle of euro notes into the passport and slipped it down the front of her knickers. It was uncomfortable but comforting. She sat on her bed until she stopped trembling. In front of the mirror she relaxed her body and made her face appear normal. Fariza resolved to force herself to go and be charming to the uncles, who never seemed to move from the salon, and then make friends with the women.

The house was dark and silent. Fariza lay fully clothed on the bed, eyes wide open. She pressed the button to illuminate her watch dial. It was three o'clock. Holding her boots in one hand, she padded noiselessly to the door. Slowly, she turned the handle and pushed gently. It did not yield.

Alice walked for the whole of the afternoon. First down to the river and along to Notre Dame, then to the Luxembourg Gardens, where, even on a freezing February day, lovers strolled and kissed. She sat for a long time over tea in the Swiss chalet, all the while trying to work out what she could feasibly do next. Emerging into the cold and dark, she found an elusive Paris cab and went back to the hotel.

From her room, Alice stared out across the street to the cemetery, which, unlike the roads, was still white with snow. She took a swig from a bottle of vodka and lay on the sofa. Someone tried the handle to the door and then knocked. Alice was not sure she could take Jamie just now, but got up and opened the door.

They fell into each other's arms. Fariza was crying and shaking, crushing herself to Alice's body.

'Alice, thank God, I never thought I'd see you again. Hold on to me, please.'

'My darling Fariza, I can't speak. I thought – or rather – I tried not to think – God, I've never been so happy to see anyone, ever.'

Gradually, Fariza's sobs subsided, her shaking stopped. She fell on to the sofa and held Alice's hand.

'Oh, Alice, I am so sorry. Thank you for being here – I feel safe at last. I'm totally fucked – a nightmare, but it's over.'

'I am just so relieved to see you. Sit down. What can I get you?'

'I must just crash,' Fariza said.

She pulled off her boots as she hopped over to the bed and slid between the sheets. Alice sat on the edge of the bed and ran the back of her hand down Fariza's cheek.

'My darling girl, whatever has happened to you?'

Fariza drew breath. 'The first thing was, I thought I'd lost my phone...'

Jamie arrived shortly afterwards. Fariza was fast asleep. They sat in the suite's small sitting room and kept their voices low.

'I've never even met the girl,' Jamie said, 'but I'm so bloody glad she's back. It was really getting to me this afternoon.'

'Jamie, you have no idea,' Alice said, and told him the story. 'Then she just fell straight asleep, so I don't know how she got back.' She paused. 'If Fariza's up for it, and I'm sure she will be after a vodka, let's go out and celebrate. I think my appetite's come back. Then we'll get the last instalment.'

'Great. Shall we go back to the Lebanese?'

'I don't think that's a great idea in the circumstances, do you?'

'I guess not. I could get us into La Mascot, totally French, not a hint of Empire, but I can't afford it.'

'Go ahead. I'm sure we'll manage.'

'There's a bar in front of the restaurant, halfway down Lepic. See you there in a couple of hours?'

'You will.'

Alice pulled Jamie off the sofa and kissed him before gently guiding him to the door.

* * *

The bar was packed and very noisy. Fariza, now looking herself in blue silk and stilettos, her black hair swept to one side, inclined her head charmingly when introduced to Jamie, himself in a sharp Paul Smith jacket and white linen shirt. They were shown to a red leather banquette in a mirrored alcove. Jamie guided them through the extensive menu. He strongly recommended they start with the fish soup and ordered a bottle of Pouilly Fuissé. The *amuses-bouche* arrived with glasses of Crème de Bourgogne. Not a cheap date, Alice thought.

'I thought you'd be so angry,' Fariza said, 'but you've been kind, and I've certainly learned a lesson the hard way.'

'Just having you back seems like Christmas to me,' Alice said, and leaned over to hug her. 'Jamie knows all about you and he's been great, so stop being such a drama queen and tell us how you got away.'

'Jamie, you're going to think I'm quite crazy,' Fariza said, looking into his eyes. She briefly put her hand over his.

'I'll let you know,' Jamie said.

The soup arrived in a tureen with rouille, croutons and a bowl of grated cheese. The waiter chatted genially as he served the soup and returned the tureen to a sideboard.

'It was a bit like the Saud. All the women covered up, but mainly with money. I did wear a scarf. No one spoke French except Amer and there were all these men in suits. They were meant to be his uncles, but it was like they were his bosses, giving him orders and looking impatient. I'm starved,' Fariza said, and for a minute was taken up with garnishing and tasting the soup.

'This is totally fantastic. It tastes as fresh as the sea. This is a great place, Jamie.'

'Thanks. I'm really glad you like it,' Jamie said, and smiled at Alice.

'Amer, who I now think of as way below a rat, wants to

take me to some sub-Saharan hellhole for a sort of marriage and I'm thinking, sure, I've got to get out of here before he chains me to a radiator and starts injecting me with heroin.'

The waiter presented three glistening grilled turbot for their appreciation before taking them to the sideboard for boning.

'Then I wait. I know I have to get out before morning. About three, I tiptoe to my bedroom door – and it's locked. This terrifies me and I freeze. Then I go to my first-floor window and there's a pipe running down to the garden, and I have to risk it. I tear my top, but I make it, and crawl out of the garden into the street.'

For a while Fariza, head down, concentrated on devouring her fish.

'I'm free, but a lone girl with a torn top in the middle of the night. I keep to the shadows and head for the centre of town. I find a taxi but the guy wants a hundred US dollars to take me to the airport, but I finally persuade him to take euros. He looked at me all the way in the mirror, and I'm imagining he's going to rape me and rob me, but he doesn't. And that's it. I got a standby without any trouble, got to CDG, bought a new phone and called home – I've got to go back for my auntie's wedding. I couldn't call you, Alice, because your number was on my SIM and I'd never memorized it. So here I am. Older and wiser, that's what people say.'

Fariza sat back and opened her arms, looking at each of them in turn.

'That, Fariza, is an amazing story. You are so bloody brave,' Jamie said.

'Bloody stupid,' Fariza said, 'I never want to be that scared.'

'I'd really like some coffee and a large vodka,' Alice said.

'Me too. That sounds lovely,' Fariza said.

'When in Rome, as my auntie says,' Jamie said, and made the order.

Later, Alice called for the bill.

'When will we three meet again?' she said, and held their hands. 'Time for bed.'

* * *

Alice and Jamie sat on the terrace smoking and drinking coffee.

'I've got to go back to London. Dad wants me to go to a trade fair in Munich with him. He used to take Mum for eye candy, but he thinks she's too old now, so it's me.'

'Pimping your daughter? Do you mind?'

'Not really. He pays me.' She put her arms round Jamie and pressed her lips against his and enjoyed the responding pressure. 'Thank you, Jamie. You've been so good. I might have gone crazy on my own.'

'I like you, Alice. I was glad to be around.'

'Keep in touch. I'm fond of cakes. I mean it,' Alice said.

'Thanks.'

They sat in silence, hunched in their coats, staring into the traffic.

'That mate of yours is really something,' Jamie said. 'In the restaurant, she's like, nothing much has happened.'

'People think she's a princess,' Alice said, 'but she's not, she's a unicorn.'

'Enchanted,' Jamie said.

A TIDY GARDEN
Annette Caseley

Five months ago, I had everything. I had toned muscles without ever having worked out at a gym, a tan without having been on holiday, keys to my ten-year-old Ford truck, a lawnmower, green rubbish bags, a spade with a wishbone handle, a digging fork, a rake and an edging knife. Amazing that I chose bare hands to execute my plan. I had a message from a woman suggesting more than a gardening job. I always have offers but I belong to Emily, and for two years I had Emily's heart. What I didn't have was what mattered the most: Emily's heart today. I wanted it back.

As we sit opposite each other, I am trying not to get annoyed at her sending text after text to her editor, Alan. I can tell that the lack of response is upsetting her. Emily says that it's about an article he's commissioned her to write, but she's lying. For months, all I have wanted was to sit here in New Zealand with her, outline my plans to leave London permanently, buy a house in Auckland and start a family. The ring is in my pocket. I need to find a beautiful and clever line. 'Will you marry me?' is too plain and 'There is no future without you' sounds desperate and scary. Her texting is shifting my attention away from my intended proposal. What she doesn't realize is that Alan won't be texting her back, not today, not ever.

We first met in New Zealand two years, three months, two weeks and three days ago. I went to the Buffalo Bar after work to celebrate my thirty-first birthday, having changed into a light blue shirt and my favourite Levi's. My brother and mates had finished singing 'For he's a jolly good fellow' when I noticed her sitting at a nearby table, looking at me.

'They're journalists working for the *Auckland Times*,' my brother whispered.

Before I could object, he'd marched me over. He knew one of her colleagues and we were introduced. Emily O'Hagan: long wavy auburn hair, freckles and green eyes – a mesmerizing combination. She was sipping white wine from her glass. Her make-up was sparse, with a touch of lip gloss. Her only jewellery was a silver bracelet round her perfectly formed wrist.

'Can I buy you a drink?' I said – a safe, reliable chat-up line. Silly really as her glass was full.

'A Chardonnay please, a French Chardonnay, not a naff Australian one,' she said.

As she sounded like a wine buff, I challenged her to a game: if she could correctly name the flavours in the wine, I would buy a bottle of champagne. I came back with a pale yellow French Chardonnay, having memorized the aromas listed on the back of the label. She observed the colour, swirled the contents round her glass and sniffed the wine before taking a sip.

'Well, I would say... spices... yellow plums... and apple,' she said.

'Crikey, you're good at this.'

I didn't point out that she'd omitted honey or that the spice was nutmeg; I wanted her to drink with me. The champagne was expensive but I intended to woo her with the two facts I knew about the famous beverage, courtesy of a brief fling with a French woman born in the Champagne region.

'Did you know that in the seventeenth century champagne wasn't bubbly?' I said.

'Well, that's not exactly true,' she replied. 'Bubbles are part of the fermentation process of wine making. One has to let all the gas evaporate to produce a "still" wine. No one wanted bubbles before the Brits developed a taste for them and eventually they became popular in France too.'

'You know heaps about wine.'

'I used to write for a trade magazine for the wine industry before I moved to the *Auckland Times*.'

I hoped I could impress her with the only other fact I had learned from my French lover. I showed her the cork that I had insisted the barman give me.

'See the comet on this cork. Do you know what it refers to?'

'Well, you've got me on that one,' she said, laughing. 'I sense that you are a bit of a connoisseur yourself.'

'The comet is Napoleon's comet. It was spotted in 1811, which was the year of a specially fine vintage.'

'Very impressive, Monsieur.'

I noticed her surprise, having observed it before in university graduates, middle-class clients and former lovers: no one expects a gardener to tell you something you didn't already know except about plants or trees.

'Well, it must be hard work being a gardener,' she said, finishing her second glass of champagne.

'You mean the physical side of it?' As she nodded, I carried on. 'That's the easy part. The hard bit is finding the courage to kill a plant or tree. For example, this morning I had to fell a weeping willow. It was a hungry, light-sapping, root-infesting tree, so I had to commit the necessary evil in order that the rest of the garden could thrive.'

By the time she was on her third glass, she talked more and the volume grew, as did her attraction towards me. She was at the stage where I hoped she wouldn't object to my kissing her. She was my special one, the one you keep for life, so when, two months after that first kiss, she applied and was given her dream job working for a London newspaper, I told her I was coming with her. My father had just died of lung cancer and I couldn't bear to lose her too.

Being back in New Zealand is distracting me. I want Emily to remember the beginning of our relationship, how she thought she was falling in love with George Clooney. I feel a slight panic when her phone rings.

'It's the office,' she says.

Surely he wasn't alive, but then some weeds never die. As she walks away holding her phone, my mind drifts to last July.

I found out by accident. After the July bombings on the London underground, I picked up her mobile when she was in the shower to make sure that she had my number saved under 'ICE' – In Case of Emergency. I was stunned to find that Alan's phone number was saved instead of mine. After that I followed him and observed his fifty-five-year-old eyes staring at the body beneath her shirt. He had a reputation and I hoped he would tire of my Emily. He took her to fancy restaurants for lunch, introduced her to minor celebrities he'd known for years – things I could never have done for her. For a newspaper editor, you would have thought he could read quickly, but he spent an eternity examining the label when the wine arrived. I loathed the way he laughed with her. I heard from her that he claimed that he would have been a Wimbledon champion had he not suffered from tennis elbow. An incredible claim for a chain-smoker to make. And he couldn't smoke Marlboro Lights, he had to have Davidoff cigarettes imported from Switzerland. I fantasized splitting him in half with an axe. There probably would have been 'POMPOUS' written in big letters on one side and 'PRAT' on the other.

I reckon their fling started about the time she stopped drinking lapsang souchong and switched to espresso. Perhaps the affair made her feel more of a woman, more sexy, more like a Parisian femme fatale. We were going through a barren patch. She went from barely having enough hormones to light a side lamp to illuminating the whole flat. Variety made her want it more. I couldn't figure out whether she saw our sex life as the 'warm-up' to some grand passion with him or whether I was the main meal, all three courses, and he was the leftovers.

I followed him and found his secret writing sanctuary, a flat, not in the country as his colleagues believed, but in London on Adamson Road.

As Emily walks back towards me clutching her mobile phone, I say, 'So, sorted out your article?'

'Well, no. It's odd.' She looks anxious, yet tries to sound indifferent. 'No one in the office has heard from Alan for over a week.'

'Doesn't he disappear off to write sometimes?'

'Well, yes, but he was supposed to be back in the office this week.'

I am irritated that she is worrying about him while she is on holiday with me. I can't help myself. This will hurt her.

'He's probably drunk somewhere with some bimbo. I caught him looking at the new girl when we went to the pub for Erica's birthday before we flew out,' I reply.

It wasn't true. He'd stared at Emily when he thought I was looking elsewhere. She mumbles something about having to go to the toilet, trying to hide her tears. Does she fear for his safety or his lack of fidelity? As she walks back from the toilets, having dried her eyes, I wonder if she has ever cried over me.

'It's really serious, you know,' she informs me. She's the one who doesn't realize how serious. 'The whole office is concerned.

They've contacted the police to report him missing.'

'Won't be long before they find him in some sleazy hotel, maybe with a prostitute. That's what men like him get up to.'

'Alan's not like that.' The force of her words shocks me.

'He's English, he's posh and he's exactly like that,' I reply.

As she struggles to find a fact to prove me wrong, I think about how she was in London. She had become more distant, suddenly irritated by my grubby clothes and my inability to fully understand her journalistic world. She struggled, not knowing which one of her lovers to choose. She wanted and needed parts of both of us: my looks and commitment versus his experience, worldliness and contacts. I pretended not to notice her impatience with me.

Emily had always reminded me of a 'Bowl of Beauty' – a flamboyant peony whose opulence and drama make it worth its spot in the garden. Pots are not recommended for such flowers as their large root systems don't take kindly to being restricted.

How could she be so duplicitous? At times, I believed this was my angel's way to promotion in the 'broadsheet world'. Because she was promoted, I fooled myself that her affair was a necessary work-related series of shags. I blamed her attraction to him on the fact that her father had walked out on her and her mother when she was two. I shared some of the culpability for their liaison: she tried to speak to me but I was withdrawn and uncommunicative, still attempting to make sense of my father's death.

But I knew I had to stop them when I saw him point to a pram in a Mamas & Papas shop and whisper in her ear while she nodded coyly. Another time, I caught them browsing the jewellery shops in Hatton Garden after a lunch at the Bleeding Heart. I couldn't let him steal her from me.

'You know I'm sorry. I've been slightly preoccupied in London these last few months. I don't want us to fight, especially not about Alan, but it doesn't help that you dislike him so much. I wish you could just get on with him for my sake,' she says.

I want to tell her that no man should be expected to get on with his girlfriend's lover, but I am not supposed to know – he is only her boss to me. I take comfort in the fact that she obviously doesn't want to leave me. So again I try to think of a suitable introduction to my proposal. I consider astrology for inspiration: she's a water sign and I'm an earth sign and it occurs to me that together we make mud. Not much can grow on mud, so my thoughts drift to the risks I have taken for her.

Alan had become like a bug trying to live off my favourite flower and I was mindful that the results of careful cultivation in your garden and in your life can be lost to predators in a short time.

The Tuesday morning before we flew out to New Zealand I drove to north London to work on Mr Langley Brown's garden. The retired High Court judge's face was flushed, but since it was always flushed, I could not tell whether he'd already been drinking. Unlike the stingy housewives in the area, he gave me a parking permit for the day without my having to ask. I had chosen him because of his location and the fact that he never had visitors.

He spent his days lamenting the fact that he had never been promoted to the Court of Appeal. I don't know whether it was the lack of promotion that led to the drinking or the drinking that led to the lack of promotion. He constantly moaned that his 'barren wife' was not here to take care of him. I realized she had not left him when I noticed her name on the urn above the fireplace. She died seven days after his retirement. I reckon she crashed the car on purpose: at least when he had been working, she had a nine-to-five break from His Lordship.

I called Emily on my mobile phone. A phone records expert would be able to verify my location, should I ever be suspected. I'd heard about this from a criminal barrister whose garden I looked after. My position logged in as Chetwynd Road, I worked until eleven. I knew he would suggest a break.

'Come on, young chap, time for a cup of tea,' he yelled.

'OK, sir. I'll just wipe my boots and come in,' I told him.

'Ah, I don't mind a button about a little bit of mud! Come on, my boy,' he said.

I put the kettle on. As he told me he'd started writing his memoirs, I slipped a sleeping pill into his cup of tea.

'That must be really hard work, sir,' I said, because I knew he couldn't remember his life.

I worried that he might taste the pill, but he drank his tea without complaint. Less than fifteen minutes later, he was dozing at the kitchen table. I changed into a hoody and tracksuit bottoms, paid for in cash at a street market, and walked through backstreets to Adamson Road. I left my phone on silent in the house. If anyone called, I could explain the lack of response by saying that I never chat on my clients' time.

The November rain kept the streets empty and gave me an excuse to cover my hair and hide my face, completing the teenage look. The few who had ventured out were too busy trying to stay dry to look around.

I arrived at Alan's flat and that's when I hesitated. Would my plan work? I didn't want my brother to have to visit me in prison. No one could prove that I had known about the affair, so motive would be an issue if there was a trial. I could kill Alan, walk back to Chetwynd Road and wake the judge. I could count on him to say I had been there all day. He would never admit to passing out that early. Then I would call Emily to log my position at Chetwynd Road again. The gardening would be finished in the afternoon. Even if anyone suspected a gardener was clever enough to plan this, no one could identify me with any certainty and there would be enough reasonable doubt for a jury not to convict me.

Yet, I nearly turned round and walked straight back to the judge's house. I thought of how much I wanted Emily. Alan was the bug who had landed on my peony without invitation and didn't know it was time to find another flower to devour. I suddenly felt indestructible, like the grass that survives typhoons when trees get uprooted.

I approached Alan's front door and pressed the bell. No answer. I rang the doorbell again and waited. On the other side of the road, a woman seemed to be weeding despite the weather. A sign on her front garden gate read 'Don't worry about the alarm, beware of the wife'. She was out there with a Great Dane. Both of them looked at me. I had to get inside the building. Next time the woman turned away, I was in. Thanks to my gardening experience, I was skilful at picking locks: I needed to be able to enter clients' houses when I had forgotten their keys or lost them; it was never good for business to admit to either. The dog's owner might be calling the police after spotting a suspicious-looking man entering a flat, but I would wait for Alan to return despite the risk.

I needed a good place to hide in the flat so I could surprise him. Maybe because I wanted to see his bed, I walked into the bedroom, and I couldn't believe what I found. Alan was there asleep.

I panicked and ran towards the front door, knocking a bronze Manneken Pis off a wooden side table. I tried to move – *come on, get out now* – but I was immobile. My brain took a few seconds to realize what was wrong: after the crash, there was only silence.

I twisted my body round and from the doorway looked into the bedroom. Alan was still sleeping. He reminded me of asparagus: a plant that doesn't like being moved, resenting it more the older it gets. *Go on, then. Go over there and kill him.* I realized he might not be sleeping. Angry, I marched over to the bed and yanked the sheets off him. His hand was on his chest, his eyes closed and the expression on his face was one of a man in some discomfort. I should have been relieved, but I felt cheated. I didn't have time to check his pulse and I didn't want to touch him.

Outside, the dog was barking loudly. Maybe leaving without a TV would suffice to make the woman believe I was no burglar. I hurried back to the judge's house, wondering how long it would be before Alan was found. The next day I was on a flight to New Zealand with Emily.

Now I can hear Emily shrieking. 'Oh, my God, I don't believe this!'

I think she is talking on the phone, then I realize that the ring has dropped out of my pocket and that she is speaking to me. She's smiling and I can hardly concentrate on Emily's words.

'Oh, I had an inkling. I even told Alan that you might.'

She stares at me, smiling, and she's waiting for me to speak. I am numb: she told Alan about my intended proposal?

She looks at me severely. 'You know, you are going to have to start getting on with Alan.'

I am confused. Of course she's waiting for me to propose. I want her to say yes, but I know that wishes are like seeds: few of them develop into anything. I start off with 'Emily, do you want to...'

'I have to tell you something important before you... I can't keep it to myself any longer, especially now,' she answers.

My heart sinks. *No, please don't tell me about Alan. I forgive you.*

'Alan...' she says. I put my hand on her mouth. Our eyes lock. She removes it, saying, 'You already know.'

'It doesn't matter...'

'Why didn't you tell me you knew that Alan was my father?'

THE WAY TO A MAN'S HEART
Ruth Cohen

Jay swayed gently back and forth in the old hammock, low slung between two ancient apple trees, and picked his nose thoughtfully as he deliberated whether or not to kill Miranda. The sun fought its way through leaves dappled with spider's webs and he screwed up his eyes, dazzled by their multicoloured sparkle. Maybe suicide would be a better option, or a fake accident. Midges enclosed him in the heavy air and as he scratched he mumbled to himself, 'Murder, suicide, accidental death,' in a rhythmic mantra until he fell into a soporific trance.

'Hey, you lazy sod, d'you want something to eat?'

Anne was standing there, looking hot and sexy, a bead of sweat on her upper lip and her very short shorts and tank top displaying her sinewy body to perfection. She had laid a table on the patio, and, neatly turning him out of the hammock with a well-practised heave so that he lay sprawled beneath it, she returned to the table and waved a bottle of red wine and a French loaf at him.

'I've been working on my novel,' he told her, and grinned when she raised her eyebrows.

They would gorge on bread and the rich rough pâté they both loved, drink most of the wine and spend the rest of the sultry afternoon making slow, sleepy love. The last ten days had passed like this, the early summer heat wave finally justifying their decision to spend the whole summer in the Devon countryside in an attempt to patch up their relationship. In exchange for free accommodation they were looking after her aunt's smallholding – 'Very small,' Jay had said, looking at its three hens, two rabbits and a goat.

'A fairy-tale cottage,' Anne had countered, pointing at the ivy hugging the doors and windows. 'There are even roses climbing up the wall.'

'Yuck,' said Jay as he carried their bags inside, ostentatiously stepping over what he hoped was mud on the dirty flagstones in the main living area and eyeing the steep uncarpeted staircase rising above him with distaste. 'Smells mouldy. There's probably a wicked witch lurking inside. Just as well you're not much of a cook. I don't suppose the kitchen is anything great.'

Then the sun had come out and they had had their first breakfast outside. That was when Jay fell in love with the goat. He had opened the gate of its enclosure and laughed as it foraged in Anne's rucksack.

'Piss off.' She had pushed it away savagely. Undeterred, the goat trotted over to Jay, glared at him malevolently and snatched the toast from his hand.

'You see!' She was triumphant. 'It's a pest. You'd better keep it tied up.'

'It's not an "it", it's a "he". Reminds me of your brother.' Jay was still laughing. 'I shall call him Fred. He's only trying to be friendly, Anne. Where's your sense of humour?'

'Really?'

She was cool. The dislike was mutual. When he had finished the toast, Fred butted Anne in the legs, causing her to scratch her hand on some thorns as she tried to save herself from falling into what remained of their breakfast.

'You can be a shit, Jay,' she said as she retired indoors.

'She's having one of her sulks. It's you and me against the world, Fred,' Jay whispered. 'You're a braver goat than I am.'

Fred had nuzzled Jay's leg and devoured his left sleeve, which was dangling from the sweater round his neck.

Now, as he gulped the end of the wine, he looked around for Fred to give him the last of the pâté. Anne straddled his legs.

'Forget the bloody goat,' she said. 'Let's go inside.'

Jay's head ached. He gave her a gentle shove. 'I'm too hot,' he said, 'and I haven't spoken to Fred all day. He'll feel neglected.'

'He's a goat, for Christ's sake, not a human being...'

'Nevertheless –'

'You think more of that fucking goat than you do of me.'

'No, I don't.'

'Yes, you do.' She laughed mirthlessly.

'You're jealous, you silly bitch.' He kissed her. 'Come on, don't be an idiot.'

He always knew when she was upset by the little frown between her eyes that presaged a vicious outburst.

Anne pushed him away. 'I know I'm an idiot, not clever, like you...'

'Oh, Anne...'

Later that afternoon she came to him. 'I'm sorry, I'm sorry, I'm sorry,' she whispered, and, pulling him to her, she teased him with her clever hands and tongue until he was fully aroused and all his doubts and irritation were forgotten.

**

The days slipped past. Fred had become very tame and Jay found he worked better on his novel if Fred was nearby, even resting his head on Jay's knee as he tapped his laptop in the garden, deconstructing a sentence here, deleting a few words there. The goat's presence relaxed Jay, to the point that he found it difficult to settle down to work without him. My muse, he called him, not quite joking, and Anne, after some early resistance, seemed to accept this, even laughing sometimes and calling Jay her old ram. 'Less of the old,' he'd grumble, secretly pleased. Anne started a painting course in nearby Exeter and this kept her absorbed, which delighted Jay, as he could get on with his own work without feeling guilty. She began to disappear for long periods, returning with what he assumed to be drawings of landscapes under her arm. He never asked to see them and she never showed them to him, but he did not expect to share his work either. This separate existence suited Jay, days spent working, walking or lazing in the Devon countryside, long sensual evenings.

One afternoon in late June Anne said she had something important to show him. Jay poured himself some beer.

'OK, then.'

'Ta-da...'

Anne unveiled a fully completed watercolour of a village square. It was set somewhere in rural France and reminded Jay of a picture he had seen of a village in the Vosges mountains. What was striking about Anne's picture, however, was that she had peopled it with figures seated at café tables. Most of them were vague outlines but one figure stood out. He had his head turned towards the viewer and with a lurch Jay recognized a version of himself. It had his black, unruly hair, wire-framed glasses and rather beaky nose. But as he peered more closely he noticed that the mouth seemed to curl in a rather supercilious manner and the eyes were curiously opaque. He didn't think it was a very good likeness at all.

'Is that supposed to be me?'
'What do you think?'
'Well, it looks a bit like me, but your perspective's not very good, and you have distorted all the figures. Perhaps you should stick to scenes, not people.'
'What are you trying to say?'
'I'm trying to be helpful, I'm saying –'
'That I can't draw, that all I'm good for is fucking and cooking.'
'Noooo, not exactly... certainly not cooking.'

That evening was hot and humid. Thunder was in the air. Anne had been aggressively silent since the picture incident and Jay was nervous. He had something to tell her, but it didn't feel like good timing. He got some cheese, an apple and a bottle of red wine (Bulgarian, he noticed absently), and took them outside. Fred was tethered to a nearby tree, his pagan eyes reflecting the yellow evening light, and Jay offered him the apple, which disappeared instantly.

'Thanks, old chap,' he murmured, snuffling Fred's head for a moment and getting his nose thumped in return.

Anne was sitting on a canvas chair, her feet up on another, reading, and did not look up as he approached, rubbing his nose gingerly.

'Drink, darling?'

She spoke suddenly.

'If you think I'm crap, why not just say so?'

'No, no,' he said. 'I didn't mean... I wish I could eat my words. It was just I didn't like seeing myself like that, so exposed. I think you have real talent.'

Jay was rather pleased with this speech. He was not normally so generous. Yet despite his appreciation of his own magnanimity, he was surprised at its apparent success in placating Anne so speedily.

'OK, I'll have some wine,' she said.

They drank together, silently. It got darker and the air got heavier. Anne lit a candle.

'I've got some news,' Jay said at last. 'My agent thinks my novel is really promising. She wants me to go to London tomorrow for a couple of days, possibly talk with a potential publisher.'

'But it's your birthday on Thursday.' It was difficult to see Anne's face. 'Can't I come with you?'

Jay preferred to go alone. 'I'll be back by Thursday, sweetheart,' he said. 'I'll take you out to dinner then. Maybe we can celebrate,' he added.

He waited anxiously for the expected tantrum. Anne rose.

'I accept the terms,' she said obscurely.

Then she came towards him and as usual her lithe body enfolding his was enough to drive away all conflict, and when the rain finally came and sent them indoors they were satiated and content enough with each other.

The trip to London was a success. Jay liked his agent, a clever woman in her fifties with a wicked sense of humour. She took him out to dinner at a Spanish restaurant in central London and praised his work. But the noise and clamour of the city disturbed him and he missed the goat, the soft Devon countryside and Anne in his bed. So he was not displeased when Thursday came. He had a morning meeting and caught the mid-afternoon train to Exeter, arriving early evening.

He had left a message for Anne, but she was not at the station, so he got a taxi, cursing mildly at the expense, assuming she had not picked up his text. Silvery clouds streaked the fields in the summer evening light as they drove along and the air was soft and clear. Perfect as the evening was, Jay was apprehensive as they drew near the cottage and his hands felt sticky. What sort of mood would Anne be in? He had forgotten to book a table for dinner and time was getting on. He texted Anne again, but she was not responding. By the time he arrived at the cottage he was sweating profusely.

'Jay!'

Anne was running out to greet him. He feared something was wrong as he paid off the taxi driver and turned towards her.

'I'm home,' he said unnecessarily, and put his arms around her. 'Is everything all right? How's Fred?'

'Everything's fine.' She smiled at him sweetly. 'Happy birthday, darling. She led Jay indoors, took his bag from him and sat him down on the sofa. 'It's a bit chilly tonight, so I thought we'd eat indoors,' she said.

Jay began to feel better. 'But I've booked a table,' he lied confidently, already savouring the seductive smells coming from the kitchen.

'Never mind, cancel it,' she said. 'I thought I'd do you a special meal here, then you can drink and not drive, and...' She stroked him suggestively.

At last Jay relaxed. This was where he wanted to be, at home, cosseted, a potentially successful writer with an adoring woman. Anne had laid out his favourite smoked salmon on a plate and a rich aroma of onion and garlic wafted across the room. Flickering candlelight hid the damp patches on the walls. Cold champagne was followed by an aromatic red. An elaborate dish of fennel with Parmesan complemented a succulent casserole. Then, the French way, a huge smelly cheese flowed on to a plate, followed by a chocolate confection that the most die-hard chocoholic could not have dreamed of.

Jay lay back, replete. Indeed he had eaten so much he felt slightly sick. 'I've never known you cook a meal like that,' he said. 'Whatever did you do to make that casserole so tasty?' He belched gently. 'Oh,' he sighed, 'I feel so guilty. I'd forgotten Fred. Wouldn't he love this? Let's go outside and give him some – a bit of the casserole perhaps? Annie?'

Anne smiled.

'You go,' she said.

A LIGHT FINGER BUFFET
Colin Harlow

'I wanted the end of August,' Valerie said, edging herself to the front of the settee, pausing over a selection of cream cakes in a Birds' Confectioners box on the coffee table in front of her and her sister Janice. 'I reckon six months after the birth is a good enough time as any. If you're lucky the kiddie isna too heavy and it stays asleep.'

Janice nodded, helping herself to a chocolate éclair.

'It's that minister's fault. We would have been set if she hadna been redistributing the collection boxes into her own pockets. Did you know she's gone and fucked off and we were put in limbo till we could have a word with the replacement?'

Janice shook her head as cream dropped on her blouse and a chocolate moustache was left around her top lip.

'September's no good for us either,' Valerie said, placing a cream slice on a side plate. 'We've got an executive cabin booked at Center Parcs.'

'And we're not around for the majority of October.'

'Exactly, and I'm not having you miss it.'

'We wouldn't,' Janice said. 'She's too adorable.'

The sisters looked over at the baby asleep in her crib.

'We met the new minister, asked him if we could request a late christening as we had his sister coming down from Southport.' Valerie took a bite of her cream slice. 'He started ranting on about how Christian values should tell us summat about compromises and that it was a house of God and not some Harvester restaurant and 12.30 would have to do.'

'That's bizarre,' Janice said. 'There isn't a Harvester round here.'

'That's what I thought,' Valerie said as she reached by the side of the settee to a pile of invitations and handed Janice one. On it was a picture of the baby and the details. 'Got them done for nowt. Bob's got contacts.'

'You're going up in the world.'

'All the way,' Valerie said. 'You can't simply tell folk on the phone – they always get the date and time wrong. This way there's no excuses.'

'No excuses?' Janice asked.

'For not replying with notes or cards.'

'You don't half do things properly, our Valerie.'

'Of course, we'll get hardly owt back from his side or his friends. They barely know how to grunt on the phone.'

'Pass us me handbag, duck. I'll scribble you a note right now.'

The invitation arrived. Sheila and Gary were invited to attend and witness the baptism of Jacqueline Louise on Sunday 25th November, ceremony to start at 12.30 p.m. It was beyond Sheila why they were calling it a ceremony. It was a christening, not the opening of the Olympics. Maybe that was how they did things, the Methodists. Sheila and her family were Church of England. This was the first time anyone in her family had decided to bring their kids up in a different religion.

'It must be all her doing. Her lot's always been big churchgoers according to me mam,' Sheila said to Gary, referring to her sister-in-law, Val.

As Sheila reread the invitation, she noted a finger buffet was to follow at 12 Oxford Street. She thought that was convenient At least she wouldn't have to get a joint in, and one thing she'd credit Val with was always putting on a good spread, even if it was down Oxford Street, a small side road that backed on to a fibre-glass factory and Bass' brewery. Not quite the middle of London's West End, like Val would have had some people believe.

'Have you seen that, what they've gone and put on the bottom of the invitation?' Sheila said to Gary. 'RSVP. What do they think they're playing at? Trying to be posh. I bet for a minute they haven't a clue what it means.'

Gary looked at the invitation. 'You probably don't either.'

'Course I do. I managed a GCSE in French of some description. Anyroad, what on earth brandy has got to do with a christening I dunna know.'

'So you won't be sending a reply card, then?'

'Don't be so bloody daft. Our Bob's already rung to ask me if I want to be godmother. I've told him yes, so they know we're going. Why on earth would I be forking out on postage as well?'

'Thought perhaps you could send one of your home made cards, so Jacqueline Louise would have a keepsake for when she's older.'

'The christening present will be keepsake enough with the amount I intend to spend, dunna you fret. And what time of day is that to be having a christening anyway?'

'It's probably the only time they could get.'

'It's probably all her doing more like. If that one's been given a choice, she'll have gone for the slot creates the biggest upheaval for us. Her lot aren't going to be up at the crack of dawn to get there in time.'

***

'I just knew it,' Valerie said to Bob as they went through the replies a month before the christening. 'Nothing from your lot or so-called friends and as expected proper replies from my side.'

Bob was putting either a cross or a tick against names on a sheet of A4 paper listing who had been invited to the christening as he and Valerie sat at the dining-room table having their tea.

'But my lot have replied. They've phoned to let me know. So have me mates.'

'You and that sodding phone. It's your best friend these days,' Valerie said as she looked over at the list. Most of her family and friends had a cross against their names. 'Have you had yer cosy little evening chat with big sis yet?'

'No,' Bob said, 'not unless she phoned while I was putting the kids to bed and you forgot to tell me again.'

'How could I forget? It's all Sheila this, Sheila that at the moment with you, Bob. You dunna seem that bothered with your Julie in the same way.'

'She's local and she hasn't had to go through what our She has. None of you have.'

'Gone through what, Bob?'

'Nothing.'

On the morning of the christening Bob and Valerie still had rolls to butter and the dining-room table in the middle room to dress for later. Michael John, their four-year-old, was trying to feed his cheese and ham sandwich into the DVD player while running round the living room wanting to play horsey and refusing to take off his pyjamas to have a bath.

'Do you want to play fishes with Daddy in the bath?' asked Valerie, trying to cajole him.

'I dun't want to be no fishy, Mummy,' he replied. 'I want to be a horsey.'

'Well, why don't you go and be a horsey in the bath with Daddy?'

'But horsey canna swim in bath, Mummy. He inna no fish.'

Valerie smiled. You clever little sod, got yer mother's brains. 'I know, why doesn't the horsey sit in the bath, pretend he's a fish-horse waiting for a mermaid to come and give him magic powers so he can swim?'

Michael John considered this carefully for a moment, his face puzzled, then he shouted to Bob, 'Hurry up, Daddy. Come and be a fish-horse in the bath with us.'

Bob pretended to trot as he led Michael John towards the bathroom and turned on the taps.

Valerie took the baby upstairs to dress in the christening gown and get herself ready at the same time. She and Bob had gone to Hewitts, the specialist children's outfitters in town, to buy it. It was an ivory silk dress with hand-stitched smocking around the bodice and wrists.

'It's a bit pricey for just one day, Val,' Bob had told her when they were out shopping.

'Course it is. It's her day, i'n't it?' replied Valerie.

'But she won't remember any of it, so what difference will it make?'

'It'll make all the difference to the photos is what.'

'Can't we get anything cheaper from somewhere else?'

'Like where? Primark, Aldi, or maybe push the boat out and see what line in christening attire sodding George at Asda is up to?'

'I was thinking more of Peacocks in the indoor market.'

Valerie gave him one of her stares. 'She's your first daughter, Bob, and you want to fit her out in something off a market stall.'

'Me mam used to buy us loads of stuff off it when we were kids.'

'She thinks you can get a complete outfit for ten pounds!'

'Well, you can off Peacocks' stall.'

'I'm having no child of mine in some tat on her christening day.'

'Can't we compromise?'

'I'll compromise. I won't have the frock if you don't have Sheila as godmother.'

The conversation was over and the gown bought.

Jacqueline Louise lay on the double bed in her new gown and a clean nappy, her fingers closing and opening into her small palms. Valerie was getting ready. She had bought herself a three-quarter-length red dress from Evans. The shop had run out of size 24s so she decided on the next one down; matched it with a black bolero jacket, a diamanté belt and new stilettos. She looked out from the bedroom while the rain drizzled against the brewery in the background, picked up the baby and sat rocking her for five minutes. She went downstairs to the lounge.

'What do you think, then, Bob?' Valerie asked, handing him the baby and giving a twirl.

He glanced at her from head to toe. 'Fat,' he told her.

'What do you mean "fat"?'

'I mean fat, still fat and getting fatter. What do you think I mean?'

'You'd be fat if you'd just had a baby.'

'You were fat before you had the baby.'

'What do you expect? I was pregnant.'

'You were fat even before you were pregnant.'

'That's because I never got my figure back after having our Michael John.'

'That's because you never stopped stuffing your chops, more like.'

'That was depression.'

'It's always summat with you, i'n't it?'

'Sometimes, Bob, all I ask for is a bit of support, but you're just like your damn father. Say it how it is.'

'Well, that's how it is, i'n't it? Now get yoursen shifted into that car.'

* * *

There wasn't much traffic on the motorway. Sheila and Gary had agreed to pick up her mam, Irene, and one of her mam's neighbours on the way.

'I'll bloody kill him,' Irene said, looking for the front door key. 'He's taken the sodding thing again.'

'Who? What you on about?' Sheila asked.

'Your sodding father, that's who,' Irene said. 'He's pissed off already with our Julie and the kids.' Irene looked in her key pot on the mantelpiece for a spare: nothing. 'You can imagine the face our Val will have on her if we're late. She'll never put that neck of hers in.'

'I know it's here somewhere,' Sheila said, as she looked in her handbag, taking out cigarettes, lighter, lipstick and purse. 'Panic over! I knew I had a spare.' Sheila handed Irene the key. 'Let's get locked up and down the church before Val gets all sweaty. You know that complexion of hers canna stand tension.'

Valerie and Bob were the first to arrive at the chapel. Valerie wanted to make sure everything was in order and get Michael John settled before the commotion started.

'Can you all sit on the left-hand side?' said one of the chapel wardens. 'There's another child being baptized today.'

'Since when has this place been doing christenings en masse?' Valerie asked.

'Since the new minister took over,' came the reply, as the warden directed them to the front pew. 'Apparently it's cost effective.'

'I inna sure about this new one,' Valerie said, undoing the buttons on Michael John's new coat. 'At least with the other one you got what you wanted, even if she was on the rob.'

Valerie looked at her watch, then leaned over to Bob. 'If she's not here by half past our Janice will have to step in.' She looked round at the seated congregation. Anybody that mattered was here and the minister was hovering by the doorway. 'I dunna care what she's been through, she's not ruining my Jacqueline Louise's day for anything.'

'Wind it in,' Bob said.

'I'm just saying.'

'You're always just saying.'

Sheila arrived at Cross Street Methodist Chapel with five minutes to spare. She was ushered to the front pew to join Valerie and Bob, the children and the other godparent, Valerie's brother. She sat next to Bob.

He gave her a kiss on the cheek, squeezed her thigh. 'All right, our kid?'

'I'm OK. Ta for this.'

'You're cutting it a bit fine, our Sheila,' Valerie said, leaning across Bob.

'You'd be cutting it a bit fine if you'd travelled half the length of the M6 for the last four hours,' Sheila said, picking up a hymn book and glancing at Valerie's red dress. 'Mind you, with that frock you're not doing a bad job.'

The minister walked to the front of the chapel, opened his arms and welcomed everybody. Valerie looked across to the pew on the right, where the other family sat. The mother had obviously gone for a cheap option: her kiddie looked to be in a nylon romper suit, as if she'd just yanked the poor sod out of his cot. It didn't look as if she had even bothered to give him a bath. She pushed Jacqueline Louise's fringe away from her eyes. She remained sound asleep.

'I'd like to call on both families to bring Kyle James and Jacqueline Louise to be baptized into our family here with God.'

Valerie, her brother, Bob and Sheila stood up and walked to the altar. The other family joined them.

'May I ask the godparents to come forward with the children?'

Valerie edged forward, holding Jacqueline Louise.

'I said the godparents, not the mother. Please let one of them bring me the child.'

A LIGHT FINGER BUFFET

Valerie handed the baby to her brother.

'Val, I'm not any good with nippers,' her brother said.

'Well, you'd better learn and fast,' Valerie said.

'Let me,' Sheila said, taking the baby from him and cradling her.

'No,' Valerie said, taking back the baby. 'He's got to learn. He'll be around far more than you.'

'Let our Sheila hold her, for Christ's sake, woman,' Bob said. 'She's only here for the day.'

Sheila smiled at Valerie and took the baby back.

The ceremony didn't last long and the baby slept throughout. Sheila attributed this to her being the godmother – the baby had obviously inherited this good nature from her side of the family. Valerie considered it a small miracle, especially with the constant cooing and mithering she thought Sheila was making around her.

'You should give motherhood a go, our She,' Valerie said as they left the chapel. 'It'd give you summat else to fill your time with besides all that stencilling you have to do on that big house of yours.'

Sheila walked over to her mam.

'You all right, love?' Irene said. 'You're looking pale.'

'Yes, fine, thanks.' Sheila smiled. 'Service wasna too long, were it, Mam?'

'Sodding long enough for those Methodists to send round two plates for collection though.'

'Suppose so.'

'No suppose about it, two families for christening, plus morning and evening services. They will have raked it in today.'

'Come on, Mam. Let's see what grub she's got laid on.'

'That terraced house in Oxford Street isna best designed for entertaining,' Irene said. 'I reckon that's why they've gone for a finger buffet.'

***

It was a narrow house, with a front and middle room, kitchen and combined toilet and bathroom – all leading off one after the other. Bob and Valerie had set up the buffet table in the middle room, so people could mingle. The table had been boxed in with a large white sheet tablecloth like at weddings. One side of the table had bridge rolls and cobs filled with ham, beef and turkey; slices of pork pie, pickled onions and sausages on sticks. On the other there were bowls of assorted salads, continental cheeses, tortilla chips and a selection of dips.

'The front room's a play area for the kiddies,' Valerie said. 'There's chairs in the middle room for the rest of you to be sitting on.'

'I'll be sitting on a comfy chair in the front room, ta very much,' said Sheila's dad, heading for an armchair in the front room. 'And I'm doing no bloody mingling for any bugger. Especially with those hard-backed chairs our Val's got in that middle room.'

'You're very welcome to sit wherever you want, Francis,' Valerie said, smiling at him and silently wishing the old fart would piss off and sit under a bus.

Bob and Valerie were circulating, asking their guests what they wanted to drink. Valerie had decided to limit the choices. It was pop for the children; tea, white wine or beer for the adults. They had bought cheap wine and beer from the Cash and Carry. 'Your family wunna know the difference and mine will understand and appreciate what a waste of money forking out on the good stuff would be,' Valerie had said to Bob when they'd been planning the do. 'Especially when they're there just to get pissed anyway.'

'What's your poison, then, our She?' Valerie asked.

'You,' Sheila said, coughing into her hand.

'Sorry, didn't catch that.'

'Have you got lager as well as bitter?' Sheila asked.

A LIGHT FINGER BUFFET

'Of course,' came Valerie's reply. 'We do have choice in this house.'
'I'll have a Mickey Mouse, then.'
'A what? We anna got time for cocktails, She. Tell her, Bob.'
'It inna a cocktail, Val. It's just half lager, half bitter,' Sheila said.
'How sophisticated,' Valerie said, smiling to the rest of the assembled guests. 'Where did you think up such an exotic gem and how on earth is it meant to fit into a pilsner glass?'
Everybody in the room turned to look at Sheila.
'It doesna,' Sheila said. 'I'll have it in a pint and dunna worry about the umbrella in it, love.'
Valerie turned, went back to the kitchen. She opened and slammed cupboard doors trying to find a pint glass. Valerie mixed the concoction. She was just about to stir it with a chopstick, when she noticed the dripping she'd left on the side of the worktop to cool off. She dipped her finger into the fat and gave Sheila's drink a quick stir.
'Here,' Valerie said, thrusting the pint pot into Bob's hand. 'She's your lot. Told you she wouldn't be a good role model.'
'Here you go, our She,' Bob said, as he handed the drink to her. 'I don't want any trouble between you two today.'
'Don't worry.' Sheila smiled at him. 'I'll be on me best behaviour. Promise.'
Valerie helped herself to a glass of white wine, a Piesporter Michelsberg – she'd bought a few bottles for herself and anybody else that might be appreciative of quality wine. She went into the middle room to talk to her sister Janice.

'Yes, we've just decorated this room. It's called Savannah Haze,' Valerie said, looking around to see if anyone else was listening. 'Bob's been up to eleven o'clock each night to get it finished in time for today.'
'He's done a lovely job, Valerie. What an effort just for us. Aren't we lucky, everybody, to be in such a beautiful room?' Janice said as she looked around the room for confirmation.

'Here, Val. What's happened to yer carpet in the kitchen and bathroom?' Sheila asked, referring to the bare orange Marley tiles there. 'Surely November's a bit early for the Mediterranean terracotta look. Even for Burton-on-Trent.'

'We had an unfortunate incident with the washing machine six weeks ago,' Valerie said. 'We're still waiting for the insurance to come through. But as usual somebody with no common sense working in an office has messed up.'

Valerie stared at Sheila.

'Ah well, saves hoovering, eh?'

'Yes, I suppose some would want to save on all the hoovering they could. Cut a few corners here and there, especially with a five-bedroom house.'

'I dunna worry about the hoovering now, Val. Not since I've got a woman who comes in twice a week,' Sheila said, taking a sip from her pint. 'It's one of my treats for working full-time.'

Treats. She should try working full-time, two kids and cleaning the sodding house.

She'd know what a treat was then, thought Valerie. The only thing that one has to worry about is matching lampshades and stencils.

Nobody had started on the food yet. Valerie tapped her wine glass. 'Bob and me haven't been up half the night preparing vols-au-vent and the like for it to go to waste,' she said, knocking back the remainder of her wine. 'So can you lot get yourselves up and tucked in.'

Valerie stood in the centre of the room pointing at the table. 'Now everything on the left is suitable for meat eaters, while the right is vegetarian.'

Sheila's dad came into the middle room as Valerie handed out paper plates and looked at her. 'Bloody vegetarian indeed, whatever next? Those daft bastards should get a life and a decent bit of steak down their necks if yer ask me.'

'Francis,' Valerie said, 'since I became a veggie I realized we can get all our essential vitamins and minerals from other sources.'

'Looks like she's been getting them from digestive biscuits,' Irene said, nudging Sheila.

'If animals are fucking daft enough to get themsens killed and eaten, it's their tough shit. I'm not having a plateful of rabbit fodder after a hard day's graft to please any bugger,' Francis said, putting two beef cobs, a slice of pork pie and a Scotch egg on to his plate.

Valerie returned to the kitchen to chat with her brothers and sisters regarding her parents' forthcoming wedding anniversary. They'd been discussing sending them away on a fortnight's holiday somewhere to celebrate. Everybody else was still sitting on those hard-backed chairs in the middle room, except Francis, who'd returned to a comfy armchair in the front. Valerie was topping up her Piesporter when she heard the baby scream. She raced through to the front room with Bob.

'We've told you before, she's not a bloody toy,' shouted Valerie to Bob's twelve-year-old nephew, Simon, who was rocking the baby. 'She doesna like to be mauled and fussed.'

Sheila came in at that moment and saw Simon fighting back tears. 'No harm done, love. Babies always cry for one reason or another,' she said, as she put her arm around him.

Valerie looked at Sheila. 'No harm done? What the bloody hell would you know?'

Sheila gave Simon a kiss on his forehead. 'Come on, love. Let's go and have some trifle.'

Valerie comforted the baby, murmuring, 'It's OK, darling. Mummy's here', and took her into the middle room to parade around her family. 'Shall we see what everyone's bought you? That'll cheer you up.'

She placed Jacqueline Louise in the middle of the room, while Bob surrounded her with the christening gifts. Michael John decided he wanted to help his younger sister and Mummy tear through the coloured wrapping paper that was in the way of the hidden treasure.

'Bob, take a picture as every present is unwrapped for the album,' Sheila said.

There were the usual napkin rings, baby's first cutlery sets – enough for an eight-place dinner party – a personalized Bible embossed in gold lettering from Valerie's parents and a crystal goblet engraved 'To our likkle Jackie Louise. Luv Nana Irene and Grandad Frank'.

'See, Val, her very own glass for when she's ready to start suppin with us down the club,' Irene said.

'Well, we'll keep it away till she's old enough to understand proper drink, shall we?'

The last present was a small teddy bear with an aged face and battered ears, lying in its box on a bed of shredded pastel crêpe paper. It was from Sheila and Gary.

'That's nice. Yet another toy for her to play with,' said Valerie.

'Oh, it's not a toy, Val. But late Victorian. Thought it would be nice if she ever wanted to cash it in when she was older. Apparently, it's quite a specialist market, antique teddy bears,' Sheila said, taking another sip of her Mickey Mouse.

Valerie stared at the presents lined up on the sideboard; her eyes fixed on the teddy bear. She gathered up the wrapping paper from the carpet, took it into the kitchen to throw away and opened the fridge to help herself to more wine.

'She's the spitting image of our Bob when he was that age,' Irene was telling Valerie's mam. 'Just like the picture I've got of him on my mantelpiece.'

'How many grandchildren have you got now, then?' asked Valerie's mam.

'Oh, just the four. Our Julie's two and Bob's two. What about yoursen, then? How many are you up to?'

'Six now, including these terror tots,' she said, as she looked at Valerie's children. 'The other two don't want any, both want to get ahead in their careers, and who can blame them? They've got far more choices than we ever had.'

Irene nodded.

'Expect your Sheila's the same. Big house and job up there in Southport. No time for kids, I bet.'

Valerie stood by the fridge door, pouring more wine for herself, listening to the conversation coming from the middle room. She slammed the fridge door, waltzed into the room, stared at Sheila.

'Time isn't the problem for that one. Actually getting pregnant is, though, isn't it, She?'

Valerie took a swig from her wine glass. Sheila looked at Bob, her face questioning his.

'Or rather getting pregnant and actually keeping it longer than four months, i'n'it, eh, our She?'

Irene got up from her hard-backed chair. 'What do you think you're playing at, you vicious cow?' She placed her hand on Sheila's. 'Why didn't you tell us, love?'

Sheila squeezed her mam's hand. 'I didn't think he'd tell either.'

The room went quiet, except for Jacqueline Louise, with all her smiling and gurgling.

THE COMMITTEE
Fleur Jeremiah

Dora was let in by a grey-haired woman and shown into the dining room. This was her first committee meeting and she felt a little intimidated by Marian, the chairman, who was standing by the dining table in a tweed suit and a frilly white blouse. The table, heavy with curved legs, was surrounded by seven matching upholstered chairs. Marian's seat, at the head of the table, was a black leather swivel chair. A murky seascape hung behind it on a chimney breast covered with stripy wallpaper in hues of green.

'Am I too early?'

Dora was anxious. She turned her gaze towards two silver-framed photographs on a dresser: a man in a tropical hat and a dachshund in a tartan jacket and a matching deerstalker hat.

'Not at all,' Marian said. 'I like people to be quarter of an hour early and not rush in at the last minute. New members in particular. And that's my late husband, Douglas – he was an anthropologist – and, next to him, our favourite dog, Frederick, also known as Teddy. Here's a little history of our organization that I wrote myself. You can keep it.'

Marian handed Dora a booklet, the print was rather faint but legible if you held the pages close to your eyes.

Dora took the seat shown to her. It was the one furthest from the head of the table, opposite a window framed by brocade curtains with tie-backs. The visible section of the garden was a jungle of overgrown evergreens and rose bushes.

'Somebody ought to do it,' said Marian firmly. She sounded and looked every inch a chairman, tall and erect despite being at least eighty.

The seven committee members remained silent. Robert, a skeletal man in an Fair Isle slipover, slumped in his chair, his eyes half-closed, an empty china cup with a rose pattern in front of him. Annie, a large woman in beige, had her gaze fixed on a plate of biscuits from Marks & Spencer's Afternoon Tea selection. Her mottled right hand, the purple hues emphasized by the paleness of her cashmere outfit, hovered above the dish. She broke into a fit of coughing. Pamela in a mauve twin set and grey flannel skirt stood up, muttering about needing the Ladies, and began hobbling towards the cloakroom in the hall with the aid of her ivory-handled stick.

'Are you telling me nobody wants to undertake this modest task? That nobody cares enough about the membership to perform this small job?' Marian stared at the man on her right.

Henry, chubby with a bushy beard, a bald head and a prominent nose patterned by broken veins, appeared transfixed by the minutes of the previous meeting.

'What about you two? You could do it together.'

Marian was looking at Judith and Rowan, a married couple. Judith, the most wrinkled woman Dora had ever seen, wore a pair of skinny jeans and a low-cut tie-dyed T-shirt. She and Rowan glanced at each other. They looked similar, could almost have been twins, each with short, silvery hair and bloodshot, powder-blue eyes. Rowan also wore jeans and his T-shirt bore an image of an electric guitar and the legend 'Rocking through the Ages'.

Judith broke the silence: 'We couldn't really take it on. What with the grandchildren and the patio...'

Marian turned to her last hope. 'What about you, Dora? You've got time on your hands, haven't you? And no role on the committee.'

'I'll do it.'

Dora had already picked up one of the brochures being handed out by the chairman in the local library. The Chislehurst Young at Heart Club had been Marian's idea. The inaugural members had all belonged to Group 77, a singles club for 'the more mature single person'. Many of those who had joined the original organization had either died or given up their search for happiness, or, like Judith and Rowan, had found it. Group 77 was down to eight members in 1995. Marian did not want the club to die altogether and decided to resurrect it under another name. In the first year of the new group, she had only two committee members, Robert and Annie, but she had saved the situation by means of a vigorous PR campaign, giving talks to the Women's Institute, Age Concern's pop-in parlour and local community action groups. She had invited the *Chislehurst News Shopper* to one of Young at Heart's events, a bring-and-buy at her house. The cub reporter arrived with a photographer and the following week's issue featured a picture of a grinning Marian, flanked by Annie and Robert, holding up a porcelain figurine of a black shepherdess. *Fun at the Young at Heart bazaar. To join, phone Marian on...* The photo and article were reproduced in the brochure, together with a detailed description of the activities on offer.

Marian's efforts resulted in a boost not only in membership but also in the number of committee members, with Judith and Rowan and Henry joining. Henry, a former curate, abandoned Anglican Church Seniors for the challenge of a new club on the condition that he could be deputy chairman, with an automatic right to succeed Marian when her time was up. The constitution was generous in respect of the length of service permitted for the officers and the committee members, and Marian was keen to emphasize the importance of continuity versus fresh blood. Hence she was still in her post ten years later, as were Pamela (PR), Robert (general duties), Henry (deputy chairman), Rowan and Judith (joint treasurers) and Annie (minutes secretary). Dora, the fledgling, had offered her services to a surprised Marian at an event on Bromley Common, where the club had a stall with balloons and a print-out of activities.

Dora had no family and Marian's suggestion that a member of the committee should send condolences to the family and friends of deceased club members appealed to her. The age limit for joining was sixty-five and the mortality rate was high. For many, the club offered the chance of a social life when their choices were restricted to the local hospital's dementia ward, Age Concern's pop-in parlour, solitude, a pet canary or grudging relatives if they had any.

Marian was all smiles when Dora said yes. Being a skeletal woman, mere skin and bones, her smile resembled a menacing grimace.

'Splendid, that's absolutely splendid. Annie, please make a note in the minutes that the club has a newly appointed condolences secretary and that that's Dora. Thank you, my dear. We will note all bereavements in the future. Not only will we be able to show we care, but we can also keep an eye on the numbers.'

'Hear, hear!' Henry shouted.

Robert opened his eyes, while Judith and Rowan leaned against each other and Annie seized a chocolate biscuit. Dora lowered her eyes.

'But where's Pamela? We need her vote.' Rowan was keen on formalities.

'I'll go and see,' Marian said, and left the room, only to return in a couple of minutes. 'She supports the motion and will be back after she has resolved her digestive issues.'

A budget of £350 per annum was promptly agreed on for the project. Marian thought it would be plenty to cover the anticipated death rate and the amount could always be revised if the coming winter proved particularly harsh. The meeting ended in the usual way, with the date of the next one fixed. No one commented on Pamela's absence as they trooped into the hall.

'Do you need to go, Robert?' Annie asked as they stood in front of the cloakroom. She felt the door. The handle was stuck.

Marian strode forth and began rattling the handle. 'Pamela, open the door! For God's sake, open the door!'

Silence.

Henry removed his corduroy jacket and rolled up his sleeves. He marched to the door, while the other committee members stood to one side. Rowan was comforting Judith, a manly arm around her shoulders. Robert held on to the hat stand, with Annie by his side. Dora pressed herself against the front door, clutching her brown curls. Marian stood behind Henry.

'Mind the plaster. I've just had the wall plastered and papered!'

'Stand back, everyone.'

Henry grabbed the door handle, placed his right foot against the wall and yanked. Nothing happened. His face was crimson and the veins on his forehead bulged. Another go: nothing.

'Pamela, are you there, dear?' Annie tried the tone she used with her grandchildren. When she employed it on the tube, other passengers wished they had chosen a different carriage. 'Sometimes non-violent methods work better.'

Henry snorted as he prepared for his third charge. This time the door handle came off and the door swung open. Pamela toppled out and lay sprawled at the feet of the committee.

Dora had never imagined that her first subject as condolences secretary would be a committee member but so it proved. Pamela could not be revived and was pronounced dead on arrival at the hospital. Marian provided the necessary background information in her neat handwriting:

> Pamela O'Donoghue, seventy-eight,
>   died in my downstairs cloakroom
>   of a heart attack on 5 November.
> She had been a committee member since
>   the beginning of the club in 2003.
>
> Pamela loved her garden and her pet
>   poodle, Truffles, who had been put
>   down shortly before its mistress died.
> She had an eighty year-old brother,
>   Anthony, with Alzheimer's in an Evensong
>   care home in Aberdeen, Scotland.
> She gave a cousin, Michael Hargreaves,
>   as next of kin when asked for the
>   purposes of an excursion.

Contact details:
5 Horton Grove, Southend on Sea.
Pamela loved the club, which was everything to her. She was also a keen churchgoer, well known to the vicar.

Armed with this information, Dora went to W H Smith in Chislehurst High Street and paused at the card shelves by 'Miscellaneous', which seemed to cover retirement, new homes, babies, christenings, thank yous, good luck wishes, confirmations, get wells, congratulations in your exams and sympathy. Should she send one to both the cousin and the brother? The address would be easy enough to find as there couldn't be many Evensong homes in Aberdeen. Dora set out to look for cards with roses, religious symbols and poodles, or all three combined, and a suitable message. In the end, she chose a cross and a climbing rose entwined, accompanied by the words 'With Sympathy', for the brother in Aberdeen and a woolly lamb against a background of hills and a sunset, with 'Your loved one is at peace at last'. Pamela's cousin might not have loved her at all, but he probably would not pay that much attention to the words.

Dora took the bus home. It was a sunny but chilly day, November at its best. The trees were still splendid in their autumn livery, the horse chestnuts of the local park displaying leaves of bright yellow and russet with patches of green.

Dora's bungalow was a ten-minute bus ride from the town centre. It was a box-like rectangle at the end of a cul-de-sac with a tidy lawn at the front, in marked contrast to Marian's messy jungle. The path to the front door was lined with rose bushes and one or two pale yellow blooms swayed in the wind. She had planted some hardy violets in the flower beds by the walls on either side of the door and they had taken well.

Sidney, her large ginger tom, lifted his head from the sofa cushion and got up to greet her in the expectation of a pouch of Felix. After feeding the cat, Dora extracted a fountain pen from a bureau in a corner and sat at her small square dining table to write the cards. With its one bedroom and combined living and dining room, the bungalow was not large enough to hold committee meetings in or to have the air of a boardroom, unlike Marian's huge house.

A couple of weeks later, Dora phoned to suggest to Marian that she put a notice in the bimonthly newsletter to the effect that the committee required a new member, but Marian would not hear of it. She said that though no one was irreplaceable, Dora's haste in trying to forget all about Pamela so quickly was 'unseemly'. The atmosphere was a little frosty at the December meeting – Marian had taken umbrage at Dora's proposal. She had concluded her opposing argument triumphantly: 'And in any case, we can't advertise because Pamela was in charge of the newsletter!'

The room was literally chilly too, it being a particularly cold December. Marian sat at her usual place, wrapped in a tartan rug, while Dora kept on her woollen coat over her lamb's wool jumper. Annie and Robert both wore fleeces on top of their usual knitwear; in addition, Robert had a travel rug over his knees and a crocheted cap which covered his bald patch.

Judith and Rowan wore jumpers reminiscent of the ones worn by the Danish detective in the TV series The Killing – the garments had slightly different patterns. The couple had confided to Dora outside the house that they took pride in not wearing identical clothes.

'We need someone to take over the newsletter. Otherwise members won't know what's going on.' Dora was being rather brave.

'Plenty of time for that. Any other business?'

'Yes, there is something.' Annie straightened her back before dropping her bombshell. 'Robert and I are getting married and we will be too busy to stay on the committee, won't we, darling?' Robert blinked, but did not protest. 'I'm so sorry, but you're going to have to find a new minute-taker, Marian.'

'Congratulations. I'm sure we'll manage. We're left with a very strong core: myself, Henry – an excellent deputy – Judith and Rowan and Dora. Dora, though a newcomer, has shown excellent promise.'

'Should I send a wedding card from the committee?'

'That won't be necessary, dear. The budget was set strictly for condolences. Henry, will you take the minutes at the January meeting on a temporary basis until we regroup? Thank you.'

Henry, who saw his position as not so different from the one held by Prince Charles, sighed.

The winter turned bitterly cold. The landscape looked stunning from the safety of Dora's bungalow, particularly when the sun came out and made tree branches glitter with frost. Sidney, old as he was, had been given back his litter box and had decided to stay indoors in a state of semi-hibernation rather than risk frozen paws. Whether Dora's roses would survive, only spring would tell. Her neighbour Will, in his early nineties, seemed to be managing – Dora caught the odd glimpse of him pottering about in his kitchen. Their kitchen windows faced each other. A couple of days ago, a huge Tesco lorry had stopped outside Will's bungalow and the delivery man had carried bags of groceries into the kitchen. He must be into internet shopping, or his son was on his father's behalf.

The Christmas concert for Young at Heart had to be cancelled. The Anglican Church Senior Singers did not want to risk travelling, the central heating at the planned venue, St Michael's, had packed in and it was doubtful whether many members would have wanted to attend. Dora wondered about the future of the group as she got on with her household tasks and was in the process of sorting out her cleaning cupboard when the phone rang. It was Marian.

'Can you believe it? Rowan slipped and cracked his skull against an icy step. I've just been told he died without regaining consciousness. Judith's off to Australia to stay with her daughter Evelyn and is unlikely to return. Make sure you send a card immediately.'

Marian paused for a while before continuing: 'It was I who found him... Such a shock. He lost his footing just ahead of me on White Horse Hill. I tried to grab him, but it was no good. He had so much to offer.' She lowered her voice. 'Perhaps too much to offer.'

'That leaves just the three of us...'

'I can bloody count! We can manage. I can manage. There's absolutely no doubt about it. I'm drawing up a new constitution that allows flexibility in the number of members. And Henry is an excellent deputy. He can do the money and you can do the minutes and the cards and odd jobs. We'll get through this!'

Dora added a condolences card to the pile of Christmas cards on her dining table. She was always careful to add a personal note to each one, so that on the card for Will she added a remark about his canary, Corleone – she often saw the bird chirping in its cage in the old man's living room and Will talking to it. For Marian she would add a complimentary remark about the club and the way it was chaired, and say how much she had enjoyed the pamphlet Douglas, the anthropologist, has written on the funeral customs of a Cameroon tribe.

The nearest relative she had was a cousin's daughter, Alhambra, who sent her a photo of a new baby every Christmas. Dora had lost count of the number of children the girl must have by now.

* * *

The Young at Heart Club was dormant for most of the winter and Marian decided to postpone the January committee meeting. A handwritten agenda arrived at Dora's bungalow for the February meeting, 'to be held at Marian's as usual at 10.30 a.m. on 13 February'. The agenda items included 'election of a new treasurer and minutes secretary' and 'adoption of a new constitution'. Dora was reading the document, scrawled on a crumpled ruled piece of paper, wondering if the meeting would be quorate, when there was a knock on the door. She was still in her dressing gown but it was a respectable one and she did not hesitate to open the door.

'Henry!'

The deputy chairman stood on her doorstep with a briefcase under his arm. He sported a black woollen overcoat, a stripy college scarf and leather gloves. He wore no hat – no need for one, as he still displayed a fine head of hair, which was unusually long for a man of his age, though it did not quite touch his shoulders.

'May I come in?'

Dora nodded silently and took a couple of steps backwards. Henry bent down to remove his shoes, huffing and puffing, his face crimson when he finally raised it and stood in the tiny hall in his diamond-patterned socks.

Henry did not mince his words as he lay into Marian and her style of chairmanship. It was time for her to step down. He, Henry, had been waiting his turn for the past ten years and it was time someone else took over. He had all the necessary qualities: he was dynamic, young for his age, had vision, knew what people wanted and could deliver, had run a medium-sized import-export business for several years and would give 110 per cent. Dora would be an ideal PA for him and club secretary, and the two of them could make the club a leading one of its kind in the country. He stood up from the settee – Sidney had vacated his usual spot and slunk into the bedroom – and towered over Dora, who was somewhat disadvantaged by her small stature and dressing gown. She managed to say that she thought they ought to discuss that and other issues at the forthcoming committee meeting at Marian's house. Henry stormed out, though his exit was somewhat slowed down by the necessity of having to borrow a shoehorn to get his lace-ups back on.

It was the morning of the February committee meeting when Dora's eye was caught by the front page of the *Chislehurst News Shopper:*

LOCAL MAN FOUND DEAD IN PARK

Henry Abercrombie, a retired curate and businessman, has been found dead in Chislehurst Park. He was slumped on a bench between the war memorial and the Venus fountain. Cause of death has not yet been established, but he may have been robbed. Papers relating to a neighbourhood organization, the Young at Heart Club, were found scattered at his feet. His next of kin have been informed of the tragic event. He was discovered by Marian Holloway, a local resident, who called Henry 'a notable member of her club, Young at Heart'.

Dora put on her good coat reluctantly. She knew her duty: she had to go and tell Marian face to face that she was resigning her post as condolences secretary, and all other posts that Marian might have dreamed up for her; in fact, she was leaving the committee and the club. She would not send any cards to Henry's next of kin. Instead she would be going to Spain for a month to visit her brother, leaving her good neighbour, Will, and his son to feed Sidney.

Spring was still some way away, but Dora could see the roses had survived and snowdrops were making their appearance. The lawn was soggy but would be bright green and ready for mowing once she returned to a proper English spring. She imagined the sound of the cuckoos, the song of the blackbirds and the loud cooing of the wood pigeons that would greet her on her return.

She rang Marian's bell. No response. She rang again and waited. Nothing.

She hesitated, then decided to walk round and find the back door. She tiptoed in the long grass, avoiding the overgrown rose bushes and evergreens as best as she could, sticking close to the wall. She tried the handle of the kitchen door and it gave.

'Marian!' she called. 'Marian! Are you there?'

A faint moaning sounded from the depths of the house. Dora stepped in and walked through the kitchen, ignoring a pile of unwashed dishes in the sink and overflowing bags of rubbish by the grease-covered cooker. She opened the dining-room door.

Marian was sitting in the leather chair at the head of the table. She had laid out the agenda and the minutes of the previous meeting at two places, while she was clutching her set of documents in her hands. She was in her tweed suit but today her hair was sticking out and she was emitting low moans.

'I'm not ready to go yet. I'm not going. You've got to wait a bit longer, Henry. Because I can do it. I am the club. Who do you think you are?'

She appeared to be addressing a faded Christmas tree in the corner with three baubles dangling from it. She then shifted her attention to a large box file on the table, opened it and tipped out the contents, so that years of minutes and agendas fell on to the carpet.

'Marian?' Dora croaked. 'Marian, are you all right?'

'Ha! Have you come to take over? You've been a committee member for a couple of months and think you know it all!'

Marian stood up, a tall gangly woman with dishevelled hair in a tweed suit and stained white blouse. She was waving a paper knife and made stabbing motions at Dora, who turned and fled.

Dora heard afterwards that Marian had had to be sedated when the ambulance came and that she had been placed in the local mental hospital. Communal living suited the woman and she soon formed an informal committee among the patients, naturally with her as chairman. Dora visited her occasionally after coming back from Spain, but she tried to avoid the times of the committee meetings. Although she wanted to warn people about standing as Marian's deputy or wielding influence of any sort in the new club, she did not see how she could convey the message and just hoped that the staff would be vigilant.

I NEVER THOUGHT THAT COULD HAPPEN HERE
Donald Clark

The protocol among cool young joggers was to be aware of each other but make no acknowledgement and Leanna Brooks was nothing if not cool, and still deliciously young, going on twenty-six. She jogged along the canal towpath in her purple Lycra shorts and black slim-fit T-shirt, white earbuds in her ears, and Coldplay blasting away on her iPod. Her honey blonde hair, tied back in a ponytail, flowed from beneath a red baseball cap. The tail bobbed from side to side as she ran. On a day like this, with the smell of the grass and the early spring flowers, the warm sun and her golden future, there could be only positive thoughts. Leanna didn't do negative and her natural disposition was rewarded by the good fortune of her life and circumstances.

You would expect the day to come to a perfect conclusion, a microcosm of her perfect existence. So when it happened, it was more than just a surprise for her, it was as if the natural order of things had been violated. The creature lunged from the waters of the canal and its long wet snout glistened in the sunlight. It sank its teeth into her right leg just above the knee and with a slight flick of its head wrenched the limb away. Then, causing scarcely a ripple in the turgid water, it sank below the surface, only its orange eyes visible. The severed leg left a trail of blood as it was carried in the creature's mouth towards Camden Lock.

    Leanna had time to look down at the stump pumping blood on to the towpath before she keeled over. She was in shock but she knew the score: make a bunched fist and press as hard as hell just above the wound. That was more effective than any tourniquet. She had learned that from her father, Jack, who had been in the Marines and knew a thing or two about people bleeding to death. He had impressed upon all three of his daughters that when it came to bleeding you had to make damned sure to stop it quick and you could never rely on other people doing it for you. So Leanna lay back semi-recumbent and pressed like hell with her bunched hand and the bleeding slowed to a trickle. Chris Martin droned in her ear. *I never knew that could happen here,* she thought.

    Within a minute or so another jogger arrived and screamed, 'Oh, my God,' and called the emergency services. When the ambulance arrived Leanna was drifting into a delirium: it felt sort of silky and fine. Around her there was now quite a crowd and to Leanna they seemed for all the world like a herd of cattle gazing with indifference as one of their number was slowly eaten alive by lions. People leaned forward and peered down with puzzled sorrowful eyes, but there was nothing for them to do, the ambulance crew had everything under control, so they ambled away. Later they would say, 'Wow, I've never seen anything like that before. She just kind of lay there with her leg twitching and then you just think to yourself: *Wow! Could that happen here?*' They would dine out on her leg, so to speak, and for a while it would be quite a topic of conversation.

* * *

The young registrar, an Indian named Patel, was on the ball. He cleaned the wound and stitched her up. No doubt about it, he saved her life. Then he went to lunch.

Afterwards she was taken to an intensive care unit. When someone experiences an event like this anything can happen, so the best thing is to hook them up to a life support system. Leanna was put to bed with various pipes and tubes sticking out of her. She was attached to cables which led to a screen in the nurses' bay just off the general ward. From this they could monitor her heart and brain functions.

By this time her flatmate, Lisa, had been alerted by the police. They had picked up Leanna's mobile phone from the hospital. It had been in her tiny knapsack, which also contained her house keys and the iPod. The knapsack had been cut off her, along with her clothes, before she went into surgery and put in a plastic bag and taken to her room. The police officers were not allowed to interview her, but one, wearing rubber gloves, rummaged around until he found the phone. From that they were able to establish who she was and where she lived and went round and found Lisa. Lisa came straight over to the hospital.

'Oh, wow,' said Lisa when she saw her flatmate lying propped up on the bed sprouting all these tubes. The room smelt of heavy-duty antiseptic and a sharp scent coming off Leanna. Leanna was barely conscious and the nurse said that Lisa could stay only long enough to establish that she knew the patient and would contact next of kin. There was a dried crust of mucus on Leanna's upper lip and her mouth hung open, her tongue protruding. Lisa noticed there were no flowers in the room and that was something she could fix right away, next time she came back.

Although Lisa and Leanna didn't hang out much, they knew quite a bit about each other and had an amiable relationship. Lisa and Leanna were in the same mould: blonde, tanned young professionals from wealthy families. Lisa didn't do negative, so she knew she could take charge of this problem. When she got home she phoned Leanna's parents in Dallas, Texas. Eileen Brooks, Leanna's mother, answered and said, 'Oh, my God, are you joking? I mean, something like that couldn't happen there, could it?' Eileen did do negative, so really she knew it had happened and a great sea wave of despair rose up and threatened to sweep her away. She felt everything else being swept away: the memories of lovely little Leanna playing tennis and coming second in a junior championship, the times at the beach when Leanna and her sisters toddled in the surf and then, when she was older, Leanna becoming a great swimmer although not the high school champion. Leanna had danced with her daddy at her high school graduation, whirling and swirling around the room in the prettiest of frocks. She would of course do the same thing, God willing, on her wedding night. But no, that wasn't going to happen now, because Leanna had lost her leg. Eileen couldn't remember what she was doing before the phone rang. All of this took a few seconds, perhaps half a minute at the most, and then she froze; she could hear Lisa still talking, but she could make no sense of it all.

Her husband, Jack, looked up from the leather club chair where he was sitting watching a ball game with the sound turned low.

'What is it, what's up?' he asked.

His wife didn't answer. She stood there with her arm crooked at the elbow, holding the phone in front of her. She was motionless. Jack went over to her. He looked back at the screen, then looked at his wife.

'What is it, honey?' he asked, then, holding her wrist in one hand, he prised away the phone with the other and put it to his ear. 'Hello, who is this?' he called down the line.

Jack didn't do negativity, but not by natural disposition.

He had learned positivity through a lifetime's practice. He had been in Vietnam. When he was platoon commander he saw one of his soldiers decapitated by a whirling piece of shrapnel that came from nowhere. Another time, flying in a Huey over the jungle, a stray bullet came through the open door and went right into the chin of the man sitting opposite. The bullet lodged in the man's head, though he didn't die immediately. There were many incidents Jack saw: blackened corpses by the roadside, flesh hanging in the trees, all these horrors and more. He decided that the only way to survive was to be positive, to believe in the face of evidence to the contrary that there was a purpose to it all. That positivity served him well when he got back to the 'world'. When he returned he went to college, was awarded a master's in Business Administration and joined a bank. Eventually, through diligence and positivity and overwhelming can-do-ness he rose to become a vice-president. Not bad going, not bad at all. Now he was recently retired, with a very handsome package of options and pension and continuing insurance benefits, and he was only sixty. Really not bad going at all. Eileen, his wife and the mother of his beautiful girls, was a pretty good partner on life's journey. Sure, she could get down sometimes, and after the second girl was born she had depression that lasted for several months. That had coincided with Jack's transfer to Chicago to run a branch of the bank. The posting had broadened his experience and cast only the faintest shadow over their marriage.

For years Eileen had been a leading member of the church choir. It was a great joy to her, belting her heart out to Jesus and him responding by giving her three beautiful daughters, and a dutiful husband and a gorgeous home. In honour of Jesus she dressed to the nines every Sunday. In summer a light cotton dress, in winter a heavy wool or even cashmere two-piece. The pastor did not approve of trousers on a woman and none of the ladies ever wore them.

Between Eileen and Jack there was something of a philosophical stand-off: the thing about Jesus is that generally he is in no hurry, so if you go for Jesus you have to go for the long game but if you want something doing quick you just have to shift for yourself, so it was no surprise that on this particular day positive can-do trumped prayerful petitioning. In double quick time Jack had booked their flight to London and a hotel, and had had a word with a senior executive from their medical insurance company.

'She's gonna be fine, honey,' he said, looking down at his wife.

He pressed the tips of his fingers into the middle of his forehead and then dragged them upwards and to the right of his scalp, stretching the skin over his eye. The eye appeared to grow large and start to pop out. It was a sort of watery blue. His hand came to rest over his ear and he gave his scalp a light scratching. His wife stroked the side of her face with her forefinger, over and over.

After she had phoned Leanna's parents, Lisa phoned Troy Keach. Troy was one of the Keaches of Cincinnati and he was also Leanna's boyfriend. Indeed he was more than that, he was her fiancé. It was a term that Leanna liked to use because although it had an old fashioned ring to it, it showed commitment in a way that was increasingly rare, but was still valued in parts of Texas and Cincinnati. It was understood, although the details had not been thrashed out, that they would marry next year in Dallas, when Leanna would almost have completed her PhD and Troy would have returned to the US at the end of his posting to London. The plan was to move to Florida, and Troy was already angling for a position in Fort Lauderdale. Troy arrived at Leanna's side just after her bedpan had been removed and the smell of it still hung in the air, overlaid with so many other hospital scents he could not distinguish between.

'Hiya, Leanna honey,' he said, and straightened the knot of

his tie. It was a beautiful silk number, Christian Dior, with little pink elephant motifs against a background of Naples yellow. With a white shirt and dark blue suit, his deep tan was set off to advantage. Troy had perfect teeth and a slim athletic build. He had an air of easy confidence, and bottomless charm. On the positivity stakes he was a champ; altogether he was very hot indeed, and his positive view of the world had been put to the test before. For a start there was his brother David. David had turned out all wrong. At school he had been a brilliant athlete and grade-A student, the usual sort of thing. He had been admitted to Harvard, but after a year, he left, for reasons he could never quite explain. Thereafter David's life became a fizzing, leaping firecracker of a thing: always jumping around and exploding. He tried poetry, guitar and performance art, working in a bookshop in Greenwich Village, dabbling in heroin and latterly working on a farm in Minnesota. He was only there for a very short while. One day he started up the green John Deere tractor and drove it over to the forty-acre field with a ditch at its far end. When he got to the field he climbed off the tractor tied a rope around the trunk of an aspen tree, one of the few trees left for miles around, then he climbed back on the tractor and tied the other end round his neck. After that, he tied another rope around the seat and then around his torso. He had thought about this, you could tell. Finally, he put the tractor into drive and headed towards the ditch. His neck gave out before the tree did and his head was whipped off and spun back into the field. The tractor continued on its own and nosedived into the ditch, with its back wheels spinning and spraying mud everywhere. It carried on like that for a couple of hours until the fuel tank was empty. Nobody ever knew why he did it. What Troy made of it was you might as well be positive. Why not? People preferred that.

Troy took a chair and sat down next to his fiancée. Leanna seemed not to notice he was there; it looked as if she was not noticing anything. She lay on her back with her head and shoulders propped on a pillow. Her eyes not completely shut seemed unfocused, the lids fluttering like wind-blown grass. Troy looked around the room and took in the metal bedside cabinet. On it were a glass vase without any flowers and a box of tissues. The fingers of his left hand drummed the top of the cabinet while his right hand rested on the bed just next to her wrist. He felt his mobile phone vibrate in his pocket. He wondered if he should stay or go. After all, if she wasn't aware of his presence there wasn't a great deal of point in staying around. He loved his fiancée, he really did, and if there was any chance of her being conscious there was no question, that was where he belonged.

'Hi, Troy,' Leanna suddenly said. 'Thanks for coming. How do I look?'

'Hey, you look great, babe, I was expecting something far worse but you look fantastic. If I wasn't already in love with you I would fall in love right now. Right here and now.'

The corners of her mouth turned up. It was a nicely understated smile. She knew bullshit when she met it and this wasn't it. She knew now that she had chosen her man well. Strong and brave, he was a partner for life.

Troy looked at Leanna. His eyes ran the full length of her body and noticed that some sort of frame affair was keeping the bedclothes off her stump. He realized that she would never be the queen bee of a private tennis club in Fort Lauderdale. This was no small matter. In the circles they moved in it was desirable if not essential for the spouse to be accomplished in a social sport. On the other hand a one-legged wife was unlikely to run off with someone else. Troy considered these two observations.

Leanna remembered a line from a Ronald Reagan movie where he has his leg removed by a vengeful surgeon. In horrified recognition of his shortened state Reagan cries out, 'Where's the rest of me?' – a line that had movie buffs rolling for fifty years. But there was no need for her to say it, she knew where the rest of her was; it was in her spirit to overcome tragedy and to be brave in the face of adversity. All things considered she felt pretty together. She looked at Troy and felt a fuzzy glow, warm and comforting. Here was the man she would spend the rest of her life with.

'Troy, I am so glad you came. We need to talk as soon as I am feeling stronger, but just for now it's great you are here.'

Her hand, lying palm up on the bed sheet, started to shift around as if in search of something. Troy reached for the hand and held it, not too tightly, not too loosely. His phone vibrated in his pocket. It was late afternoon now and through the window he could see the sun leaving an orange glow on the roofs and treetops. In the corner of the window a fly was buzzing, desperate to get out before it died. Several of its mates had already collected belly up on the window ledge.

'Honey,' said Troy, 'I was told you mustn't get overtired. I suppose I better go now, but I'll be back again tomorrow. Same sort of time.'

He leaned over to kiss her on the cheek and breathed in the sharp smell. His lips lightly touched her cheek, Her eyelids fluttered a little more rapidly. He left and in the lobby he answered his phone.

Jack and Eileen looked at their daughter, now propped up and wide awake. 'Hi, Mom. Hi, Dad,' she said brightly, like she was still their little girl sitting up in bed on her tenth birthday. On that day they, the whole family, Mom, Dad and the two sisters, had burst into Leanna's room crying, 'Surprise!' and bearing gifts of candies, T-shirts, combs, brushes and tights. For some reason this was never repeated with the other sisters, but for Leanna it marked her out as someone special. A state she tried to live up to for the rest of her life.

Eileen suppressed a sob at the sight of her daughter. She noticed the empty vase on the metal cabinet. The parents sat down on either side of the bed; each held one of Leanna's hands. Jack pumped positivity and Eileen pumped Jesus, and the two forces combined in Leanna to bring a beatific smile to her face.

'We're so glad we could get here as quick as this. Your dad did marvels getting the flights organized and we have got the most marvellous hotel. Well, it's right up the road from the Natural History Museum and all those places,' said Eileen.

'That's good, Mom. You really must make time to visit all those places while you're here. One of my favourite is the British Library, although I've kind of gone off the canal walk.'

Leanna chuckled at her small joke. As she did so the monitor taped to her chest trembled slightly, sending a heightened pattern to the screen in the nurses' bay. The temporary change went unnoticed.

Jack Brooks recognized and approved of his daughter's brave effort. He held her hand even more firmly. It was another warm day and the two hands, now moist, slid together. He curled his fingers into hers and looked out of the window.

'Troy been here yet?' he asked with a gruff note.

He wasn't sure what he made of Troy. Was it just proprietorial or was it paternal feeling that made him think that his prospective son-in-law was something of a creep? The boy seemed so sure of himself and he had never served. On the other hand that was quite normal now. What young man had served? And wasn't it a good thing that he was confident? That was certainly a quality to be approved of and his professional prospects were excellent. Probably a relationship of jocular sparring would be the best outcome. But frankly, could he be counted on to do the right thing by his now damaged fiancée? And was it fair to ask him to? A guy like Troy...

'Yes, Dad. He was here last night and he is going to be here again today. He is so busy, poor baby.'

Eileen Brooks looked down at her daughter. She knew that the bruised apple in the box always gets passed over, no matter how juicy and sweet most of it still is. She wanted to stroke her daughter's brow, but such a gesture might seem like a suggestion that her daughter was no longer free and independent. The mother knew how important it was to ensure that personal space and identity be preserved. Demonstrations of affection, necessarily unbalanced between a parent and child, could so easily create the belief that the recipient was being robbed of dignity, rather like those African tribesmen who believed that by being photographed they lost their souls. The mother's hand hovering over the daughter's forehead was withdrawn.

'Well, little lady,' said Jack Brooks, 'we're gonna have you fixed up in no time at all. We'll have the finest medics working on you and they'll soon have this little problem licked. Hell, back in 'Nam I saw some things that were far worse than this and they got those fixed up real good. We had some damn fine medics in the service, you know, and by Christ nothing is too good for my little girl. Just as soon as we can we're gonna take you back home.'

The daughter smiled up at her father. How she loved and worshipped him. There was no barrier here. She felt as if she could dissolve into this brave, strong man and their two contiguous beings would merge, like the sea lapping at the sand. With her mother she could never feel like that: her mother was cold and did not demonstrate affection, never stroked or cuddled her now that she was an adult.

If Troy was even half the man her father was... but what was she thinking? Of course he was... he was almost as good as Dad, although of course nobody would ever be as good as the real thing.

The afternoon passed with the three of them musing on private thoughts, chatting intermittently about family and friends and the house back in Dallas, or how Leanna's PhD thesis was going. Occasionally Jack gazed out of the window for long periods, and his wife bit her lower lip while Leanna dozed. Fly corpses continued piling up on the window ledge. Sometime in the late afternoon one of the nurses came in with the message that a Mr Keach had phoned to say that he had been called away on business and wouldn't be able to come until the day after tomorrow or the day after that. Leanna smiled and thought how considerate of Troy to let her know so that she wouldn't be worrying about him. Her mother's image of the bruised apple was replaced by a picture of a peach, its beautiful golden down marred by a dark slimy lesion. Her father's jaws clamped together tightly, the tendons on his neck standing out.

Finally Leanna said, 'Mom, Dad, it's time for you to go and get some sleep. I hope you can come back tomorrow. I'll still be here – I'm not going clubbing.' She gave a little giggle, girlish and tinny.

The parents rose, not looking at each other, both so weary: the effect of their journey and the unceasing struggle to make their philosophies work. At the door they turned to say goodbye to their beloved daughter and to assure her they would be back bright and early the next day.

'Mom, Dad, I'm not unhappy, you know,' Leanna said.

Later another nurse, from the night shift, came in to say that someone called Lisa had left a message that she wouldn't be able to drop by for a couple of days but for Leanna not to worry because everything was fine with the flat.

As the evening slipped into night, Leanna became aware of the sounds you hear only in institutions: strange, unexplained bangings, disembodied voices, rumbling trolleys, all echoing through shiny painted corridors. It is the echo which makes you understand you are not at home, that you are in an adjacent land, where familiar things can be glimpsed but not held, and the scents and sounds, no matter how kindly, are forever foreign. She could hear someone sobbing, perhaps at the end of the corridor, or in the room next door, or even in her own room. She could not be sure.

Later still the night nurses sat in their bay munching a chocolate cake donated by a grateful former patient who had dropped by in the evening. None of the nurses knew the donor, but they accepted the cake anyway. They still had another three hours or so of their shift to go, and this was the best time, when all the patients were asleep, or tossing around fitfully and didn't need any special attention. None of them saw the mouse, which had been born in the hospital and lived all its life there, scuttle along the corridor and into Leanna's room. The mouse sniffed around the machine by Leanna's bed. The machine was still connected to her body by a dozen different wires with rubber suckers on their tips which were kept in contact with her flesh by strips of sticking plaster. Grey cable running from the base of the machine disappeared into a run of trunking and re-emerged in the nurses' bay. The mouse, searching for something to nibble, gnawed all the way through the cable and broke the connection. Mice do that sort of thing, although it rarely brings them much benefit. Feasting on the chocolate cake, no one in the nurses' bay noticed the screen go blank. By the time they had noticed and one of them went to investigate, a tiny clot of blood had detached itself from Leanna's wound, travelled through her arteries and blocked the flow to her brain and she was already dead.

The next day Jack Brooks took charge. He was assured that the body would be released when there had been a post-mortem and he would then be free to have it flown back to Dallas. There was nothing else to be done for the moment. He would return to Dallas, organize his lawyer and sue these Limey bastards for every penny and then some. Jack and his wife sat in business class as their plane taxied for take-off. For the first time in days it rained and little drops trickled down the window. Somewhere else Troy's phone vibrated in his pocket.

BIOGRAPHIES

The Blue Room Writers first met in a novel writing workshop at the City Lit. They now get together fortnightly in the Blue Bar at the Royal Festival Hall to discuss and critique each other's work.

Peter Bunzl has always been interested in telling stories and has a background in film and animation. As well as animating on two BAFTA winning children's series *(Yoko Jakamoko Toto* and *The Secret Show)* he has written and directed several successful short films. Recently his stories strayed from screen to page and he found he enjoyed this challenging new way of storytelling. He is now working on a debut novel: a steampunk tale for children featuring murder, mayhem and mechanical robots. You can see more of his work at his website: *peterbunzl.com*

Annette Caseley used to be a high flying city lawyer but got fed up with the truth always getting in the way of a good story. She sets the rotas and organizes the meetings for the Blue Room Writers. Brought up in France and Holland by an English father and a German mother, as well as living in Spain as part of her law degree, she is truly multi-cultural, or as her husband describes her: *Eurototty*. She now combines her love of fiction with supervising her two daughters in North London.

Donald Clark began writing ten years ago after a varied career working on building sites, as a trade union official and then as a teacher. He is interested in the short story form, and has been published in *Between the Lines*. His work ranges from magic realism to examining the solitary nature of urban society. He is working on his third novel, a psychological thriller set in war time Berlin. He lives in North London with his family.

Ruth Cohen returned to writing after she retired. She has written short stories and flash fiction, and been published in the *Greenacres Writers Anthology*, which won third prize in the NAWG, Denise Robertson Group Anthology competition 2012. After reading English at UCL she became a careers adviser with the ILEA, subsequently heading up services in the University of the Arts and City University. She is currently attempting her first novel.

Colin Harlow spent his formative years in the East Midlands edged between Nestles' coffee factory and the breweries of Burton on Trent before moving to Switzerland. He trained in Dance Theatre at The Laban Centre for Movement and Dance where he was a scholarship student and recipient of the Simone Michelle Award for Choreography. He currently lives in London and divides his time between being on a yoga mat, writing and working in metal tubing.

Fleur Jeremiah has done a number of language and literature related jobs: she has been a linguistic abstractor, a librarian, a language teacher and a translator. She is a published translator of literary fiction and has evolved as a writer in her own right. Fleur spent her formative years in Finland and her background is reflected in one of the stories (*Vanamo*) included in the collection, as well as in the novel, *True Finns*, she is currently working on.

Edd Phillips is a martial arts instructor for the Rose Li School and a part-time London tour-guide. He is interested in the way the world is experienced through different perspectives and enjoys playing with and bending those perspectives through magical realism. He has written a number of short stories – one of which came first in StorySLAM (a stand up short-story reading contest) – and is currently working on *The Root Tattoo* a novel for young adults.

After a career as an anthropologist **Paul Yates** took to heart the observation of a senior colleague that – we are all basically novelists – and began to write fiction. Something he continues to do with growing relish.